FLICKER

Carlos Quiroga

FLICKER

DOUBLE DRAGON

Chapter 1
Imprisonment

The soft beep repeated itself, a beacon summoning Horatio. He moved slowly. A ghost haunting empty, dimly-lit corridors lined with processing machines. His watch stuck at a lost moment in time, he had no idea how long he had been searching. The immensity of it all gripped him with equal parts despair and trepidation. Hallways hummed endlessly as he passed. It faded into normality, and the chill of the super-cooled air had finally lost its sting. The fog of his breath provided a reminder that he couldn't continue his search forever. Though he would.

His leg muscles writhed painfully beneath his skin. Only sheer willpower forced him towards the solitary beacon. A faint whisper when he started, now drummed into his head. The fiery pain finally relented when the rows of electronic archives opened into a large storeroom. Fifty metallic egg-like pods sat perfectly aligned in five rows. Only one was active, the beep called out its monotonous song, echoing in the space. Horatio let loose a long sigh, he moved quickly to the container. The touch of his fingers on the front panel and the silvery surface cleared. A diagnostics display appeared in a transparent green hue. Horatio stepped back at the sight.

He lingered for a moment, seized by doubt. *Should I tell her? Does she want to know? Is that even her?* The last thought sent a jolt of guilt down his spine. He moved quickly, shrugged off his backpack, and pulled out a crowbar. He pondered only momentarily the dangers of prying open the high-voltage device, but the constraints of time had forced his hand. Red triangles, and ominous warnings filled the screen. The harder he pulled the more the screen glitched with static. A thin seam down the middle of the egg gradually began to give way. Horatio continued his struggle. *Crack.* A sudden electric jolt coursed, and Horatio felt his marrow sear. Pain rippled throughout his back as he hit hard against the egg behind him. Thin tendrils of smoke wafted from his body.

The left side of the pod continued to extend open, letting wisps of cryo-air skirt out along the edges. Horatio fought to maintain consciousness, slumping to his hands and knees. The pain traveled at lightning speed over every inch of his body as he tried to breathe. Horatio fell to his side. Stuck, unable to move. He groaned, writhing painfully as the smoke began to dissipate. The acrid odor of his flesh caused bile to dance feverishly in his stomach. "Mira," he coughed out. "Mira!"

"Horatio?" Her voice soft enough that it could have been his imagination, he questioned her name again. "Yes, I'm here, where are we?"

"We're at a processing center."

"The Processing Center, still?"

"No, a different one..." Horatio trailed off for fear of her response.

Mira looked down at her body, covered by a white cloth. Slowly she lifted her right arm from under the sheet. Smooth almost ivory-like skin greeted her view. She felt no sense of weight. Her breath caught, her eyes began to sting. *Please, no please,* she thought as she raised her left arm from under the sheet. Mira hesitated before finally turning her wrist. It wasn't there. Disbelieving what her eyes told her, she uttered, "Where's..."

Horatio knew he was too late to stop the process. He hobbled to the container, using it to prop himself up. "I'm sorry Mira, I tried, I swear to god I tried." He faced her now, peering into the snow-white interior of the egg, against which Mira's aquamarine hair stood in stark contrast.

"Where's Lao? Where's Neikia?" Horatio broke eye contact, and his silence only served to stoke her growing anxiety. "Gwendolynn? Jason?" Oil began to well in the corners of her eyes, sliding down her cheeks in branched black rivers. Midnight tears traced their path onto the white sheet. "Oh, God..."

"It's just us," he said as gently as he could muster, but Mira only vaguely heard his words. Melancholy had already begun to consume her thoughts. *I'm one of them.* Moments passed, the tears stopped, but the thought stabbed her repeatedly. She raised her head and her luminescent eyes bore into Horatio's like radioactive emeralds.

"You mean it's just you. I'm dead Horatio! Whatever computer, AI, technology that's running here, in me, is just an imitation. You may as well be talking to yourself right now. For all we know this is a trap, they could have complete control of me, just waiting to infiltrate," her eyes narrowed at being cut off.

"Infiltrate what? There's nothing left! Game over! My only duty was to save my leader. I just wanted to stop this, I thought I could reach you in

7

time. I didn't, but whatever is happening here, this is different. I forced the egg open mid-process." Even as he spoke he couldn't help but let a portion of his thoughts be swept up by her eyes. Vibrant concentric circles that moved in little bursts, their clock-like rotations mesmerized him. He released his grip on the egg, finally able to stand on his own and take a few unsteady steps backwards.

Mira's intensity was all-consuming. Unable to resist the pull, her eyes probed his as he continued to protest. The distance he had just put between them made no difference. His pupils stayed still, and her consciousness flooded with new thoughts, insights that could only be likened to intuition. She knew he was being honest. Mira sighed in her head, and assessed him anew. He still wore his usual tattered black suit coat, green t-shirt, and jeans. Grey dust caked over most of his body. "You're right, maybe all's not lost. We've never been able to demonstrate that the Apothites have consciousness, or something that resembles consciousness." Horatio's doubtful look wasn't lost on her. "We have to be realistic Horatio."

"We can debate your personhood status later. Right now, we have to get out of here."

"If this is a typical Processing Center, it should be connected to a Temple. Given my current appearance, blending in shouldn't be a problem. Neither should blending out."

"Right out the front door?"

"You don't think we look like the Temple type?"

"Fortunately for us, there's no longer any *type*. Let's go."

Clutching the tear-stained cloth against her body, Mira stepped out of her egg. There was no feeling of gravity to her body, she felt nothing. A limitless pool of strength was at her disposal, but the cost was a terrifying sense of disassociation from her own body. There was no anchor to prevent her from floating away from this imitation of reality. She could feel herself in a million places, a million versions of her coalescing into one, before scattering out again. Her memory was now utterly comprehensive, so much so that she risked losing herself in time. Mira closed her eyes, her legs wobbled and she clutched a nearby egg for support. A swirling vortex of thought threatened to whisk her away.

Horatio reached his hand to Mira's shoulder. At his touch, her eyes opened, the swirling eddies of her consciousness calmed, and everything focused. A smile crested her face to reassure him, and herself, she was indeed in control again.

"Here, I found a Temple uniform for you. It's not your clothes, but it'll do the trick." Mira stretched out an arm to accept a uniform-tight pink dress and neon-blue flats. Horatio turned his back to allow Mira to dress. She thought the modesty a little ironic considering that her current body had already been seen by most of the world.

Once properly attired, the two made their way through the dystopic labyrinth. The broken egg had alerted the facility, and frequent small security patrols forced them to duck in and out of corridors to evade detection. Before long, a chiming sound claimed their attention. "An elevator," Mira noted. A small nod from Horatio. They rushed toward it, clinging close to the walls, allowing a patrol to pass by without being detected. Mira waved them forward, and they crept behind the patrol as it continued forward.

Mira glided with ease soundlessly. Horatio, however, felt waves of anxiety that hampered his movements. He held his breath, and didn't dare touch the beads of sweat that tracked his cheeks. The patrol clicked on their lights as they moved into the rows of process servers. The elevator doors closed behind them.

"There's a walkway to the Temple on level ninety-six," Horatio said. as he hit the corresponding number, short of breath as if he had just run a sprint. Mira looked at him puzzled, she wasn't out of breath. Mira realized she wasn't breathing at all. Her eyes stung as she moved quickly to the window. She forced unpleasant thoughts from her head, and began to plan.

Horatio felt overwhelmed with doubts. She seemed like the Mira he knew, but was she? Did it even matter? He had nothing left. As the elevator ascended, they rose over the majority of buildings. The light of the moon added faint illumination, and he could see her reflection the glass as she peered out. For the first time, the changes in her appearance became apparent. Flawless skin, oversized digital eyes, and pony-tailed blue hair. He could no longer pretend otherwise. Mira was clearly an Apothite, one of the millions created. There were variations, but she was the most sought-after model on the market. Had he purchased her in a forgotten and misguided impulse? *Could that have happened? Worse, could I have been the captured and brainwashed one?* Finally, Mira returned his gaze. Her eyes, and brows furrowed in determination. An expression unknown to the Apothites.

"I feel wrong."

"Wrong?"

"I feel like I'm going crazy."

Horatio crossed his arms, and backed against the wall to stare out the window looking at the buildings and lights of Scelus, home to all. "If it makes you feel any better, so do I."

***

"Report."

"The Mutinist escaped with the help of a teammate we believed to be dead."

"Believed?"

"He was the one who stayed behind to detonate the explosives. There was no way he could have survived."

"Well, apparently, he did," Gustav said absently as he observed the egg. "I assume he boarded the train from the other center?"

"Most likely. We have the entrance completely sealed off. There is no way they're getting out of here." Gustav nodded in agreement with the assessment of his subordinate.

"I highly doubt they'll attempt to leave through the front entrance," Gustav said. But there was an almost unnoticeable trace of doubt in his statement when he noticed the indentation Mira had left. *How did he break her inhibitors?* "But, we cannot afford to discount any possibility. Have your men cover all possible egresses."

"Sir," five soldiers answered before filing into the elevator in mechanized order. Gustav entered, about-faced, and stood stoically, hands behind back. His mind was, for a moment, irritated by the absence of cameras inside the elevator, but he understood the need when dealing with people like the Mutinist.

"Are we sure there's only two?"

"The rest of the bodies have been recovered. They're too far past expiration to be processed. what should we do with the remains? These two are the last operational cell. They have no allies."

"Best not to underestimate two people who can walk away from death. Dispose of the bodies, throw them in the dump for all I care." The elevator lurched to a stop, Gustav led his team to the exit. "Pierce, Frie nobody gets through these doors alive."

"Understood," the two said in unison as they took their position on either side of the doors.

Gustav considered himself to be a man of knowledge. While half of the force spent their FR credits on stims, dims, and loopers the other half leased a bot or "lived" at the Temple. Although, he could understand the allure of both, he knew these were useless pursuits. They didn't know they could double their income with proper investments into certain Temples. No idea the harvest moon hung in the sky tonight. And they had no clue that this was misdirection.

Gustav scanned the entrance to the Processing Center, where trash moved listlessly with the wind. The homeless laid in their usual spots against buildings, those who were missing identifiable only by the slightly cleaner spot in the grime covered stone walls. The monotony of their day led most to lying on the ground across from the Temple, fantasizing about the time they spent inside. For now, they were confined to the "Land of the Free," or so it was called by the civilized. People traveled so little that many felt what was it to give the have nots the sidewalks. Theirs to have, at the benevolence of the haves.

Finally his sight fell on one clearly dead, sprawled out half onto the street. The blood on his head, and the small puddle underneath, were practically black. It had been awhile since his murder. "Carthy, Janic, Misant. Go to the temple entrance and stay there until I order regroup."

"Sir," they said as they moved to their new position. Gustav, nodded to himself. As he suspected they were going to exit the front door, he went back inside. Took the elevator up. There was no use for his team, the dossier he had obtained a while ago told him that much. M7 had died a long time ago, and M1 was a piece of junk now.

***

The glass walkway suspended them over the neon-ized city, above a cloudless night that made Horatio yearn to reach out and touch the moon. "It's beautiful," he said.

"Yeah, no birds though, but I guess it's fine on its own lifeless virtue." Her statement caught him off guard, but before he could probe she asked, "Do you really think there are bird zones?"

"Sure, if birds can live in the middle of the ocean."

"But what would they eat?"

The joke turned sour for Horatio. "Never going to get a view like this again."

"If we're lucky," Mira said with a smile. Horatio returned a half-hearted smile of his own. *We can barely stay alive, how are we going to end this.* "Alright, just play it casual. Stick close, if anyone asks I belong to you."

"You got it."

Mira was pretty sure she no longer needed to breathe but took a deep breath of reassurance regardless. She had never been to a Temple before, and now she wanted nothing more than to keep that record. Music pulsed the door, or that might have been in her head. As she reached, for the handle she hesitated, Horatio grabbed her wrist.

"We don't have to go in. I'm sure we can go back, and use the no cameras to our advantage."

She let the moment hold only a second. "Take your hand off of me, and enter this Temple. That's an order."

Horatio met her stare as he released her arm. "I didn't mean disrespect, I just saw..."

"I hesitated because why would a sex-bot enter anywhere. I'm supposed to be a follower now, remember? That's why I ordered you to go first. Now please, time is sort of the essence."

"Understood." Horatio darted his eyes in embarrassment as he moved past to open the door.

14

Chapter 2
Pious Duplicity

Horatio opened the door, the electronic beat flooded over them. He felt it in his chest, deep pulsations that threatened to choke him. Mira's eyes trembled to the beat for a few moments before stabilizing. Soft purple and sharp pink hues illuminated the Temple in chaotic bursts. Horatio's eyes glazed over. He'd never been inside a Temple, and the vaulted ceilings held him in awe.

In the Living Sections, the architecture was brutal and standardized, and he'd never before seen anything like this. The variations were unknown and alien to him. Thankfully, the acoustics of the structure amplified the music to such an intensity that their entrance went unnoticed. Horatio moved slowly, unaware he was in a daze as he drunk in the outre show that laid before him. Every possible sexual deviation was on display, either on wall sized screens, intimate one-on-one encounters, or the large stained glass windows that lined the entire eastern wall.

The screen displays held groups of six to eight people. Each with one hand on a device they would occasionally speak into, and the other hand on their genitals. As some would scream in ecstasy and leave, more would simply begin again. Their hungry intent not satiated in the least. Others still simply looked meditative, a slow cadenced beat accompanied with deadened eyes that reflected the light of the screen.

Bots that looked exactly like Mira sang and danced, their legs kicking out in unison and with smiles that seemed almost genuine. They laughed and bounced in a routine choreographed to the blaring music. As they threw out their arms, one of the bots suddenly glitched, statically repeating the first syllable of her word. Almost without missing a beat, a bot-dolly appeared from the wings, mechanically latched on to her and carried the malfunctioning bot from the room.

Horatio's attention was diverted by noises coming from the one-on-one shows where sexual depravities reached the extreme limits. Purchasers of the sex-bots spoke into their hand-held devices, and the sex-bot would instantly respond to any demand regardless of how debased. The seemingly endless menu of indulgence catered to every sexual appetite imaginable (and some beyond imagination entirely), running the gamut from cigarette snuffing, defecation, necrophilia, to orgiastic cannibalism. One woman lay splayed on a nightclub style table, her chest cut open. Her deadened eyes looked into Horatio's as a man sat over her holding a knife and fork. Lights danced over the scene. He cut, she whimpered. Her eyes cut through Horatio.

At this point, Horatio made a conscious effort to close off his mind into tunnel-vision mode, knowing there was no other way to make it through with his sanity intact. He pushed his way past denizens to get to the door on the opposite side of the room. The last vision made sweat exude from his forehead, he felt he was going to throw up. He hard-swallowed bile with every step. Almost like a guardian angel, Mira suddenly appeared beside him and grabbed his hand, "Come on."

Together they moved quickly through the crowd. People flooded them. "Hey, the door's this way." Horatio said with a pull, but she continued to guide him in a different direction with her immutable strength. Horatio felt powerless to resist as she sat down at a wraparound sofa in front of a screen show. There was just enough room for her to squeeze-in, between an elderly woman working a silver dildo in and out of herself and an obese man that breathed as hard and heavy as he rubbed himself. The fat man's aroma of sunbaked fish sent bile racing again to the back of Horatio's throat as he remained standing.

A flash of a smile touched Mira's face before she reached up her pink flowy temple dress. Horatio stared at her dumbfounded for a moment, before he jumped up. "Mira! Mira," Horatio yelled out in an effort to find the real Mira. It was done. Everyone started looking at him, he wasn't one of them. He wasn't a deviation exploring his path. Well he and Mira were deviations, probably in the truest sense of the word, but their paths were not in this Temple. An uproar from further inside the holy grounds alerted him that Mira had broken her cover as well.

***

Gustav found it impressive two people knowing they were being hunted didn't take greater precautions. Though in their defense the harvest moon was also known as the hunter's moon, and it had been nothing for him to track the fugitives' journey from the skywalk, and into the Temple. As a matter of fact, Gustav stood only a few feet behind his quarry who seemed paralyzed by indecision. A sex-bot walked in front of Gustav, momentarily blocking his view. Gustav seized the bot's comm device and ordered, "Grab that man's hand, and take him to watch a show."

"Two charges," the comm chirped out.

Gustav touched his wristwatch to the device, and replaced it. The sex-bot approached Horatio without hesitation and took his hand. As Mira reached out to intervene, Gustav stealthily approached her from behind and touched a silver cylinder against her neck.

Mira's eyes went static, she couldn't grab Horatio. She couldn't scream or utter even the slightest sound in protest. She was completely paralyzed save for the shivers that danced up her mechanical spine as Gustav spoke, "Hello Mutinist." Mira's body crumpled to the floor in a heap as her mind fought in vain to regain control over herself.

"I don't know how you broke free of your inhibitors, but we'll remedy that soon enough," Gustav intoned in an almost soothing voice. Mira's eyes closed, the fighting stopped. She labored to focus her remaining energy. Visualized her fingers moving, but had no tactile confirmation they were obeying. With a cry she grabbed out, reached out for anyone.

Now it was Gustav's turn to be stunned into paralysis, Mira's hand latched onto the wrist of another bot. This should not have been possible, but the reality was undeniable. Gustav noted the immediate effect Mira's touch had in the eyes of the other bot. The formerly dim turquoise-tinged orbs became vibrant emerald beacons. *This could happen only if the bot had independently initiated its own processors!* The bot's face flashed with what could only be described as genuine shock, seizures gripped its body. *This isn't their shock program*, Gustav though in panic. The female bot's head turned and, as the tremors faded from her eyes, took in Gustav and Mira with an expression of newfound revelation.

"Please," Mira whispered. A desperate plea so quiet it couldn't be heard over the music.

Gustav flew back a few feet. Blood gushed out of his nose as he rolled to his hands and knees. He was up in a moment, like a boxer recovering from an unexpected blow. He rose, staring at the bot. He only pondered for a moment, before fleeing in the opposite direction. Adrenaline moved him, checking men and women out of his way. It would be suicide to attempt to go up against a bot alone without a weapon, and there was no time to call in for reinforcements he reasoned in his mind.

Mira, slowly emerging from her daze clutched onto another bot to hold herself up. Again, the effect of her touch had similar results in the other bot, its eyes became fire. Mira could finally stand on her own, filled with a newfound sense of confidence and strength of purpose. She made her way through the crowd like a mystical prophet touching everyone she passed, mechanical and human alike.

The club began to vibrate with a different frequency than before. Loud music, and pulsating lights added to the confusion. Mira almost felt drunk as she moved through the crowd with her outstretched hands, ignoring the occasional odd looks and irritated scoffs when she came into contact with a human, but they were not her targets. Each bot she laid hands on, easily more than half the crowd, had the same immediate effect of freedom to Mira's touch. The sound of screams began to overtake the music.

Sex-bots at first moved in chaotic fashion, like marionettes with their strings cut. Within a short time, however, these uncoordinated movements seemed to come under control, bot by bot. Mira had never before seen or heard of anything like this, and she had kept up to date on every piece of robot news since she was a child. The closest thing she could remember was a nearly forgotten legend of a renegade cyborg from long ago. Mira could pick out Horatio's voice from amidst the clamor, and she headed towards him. There was no need for discretion now. The Temple had become a scene of bedlam.

Mira gazed around at the maddening crowd as she made her way to her destination. Violence had already begun to erupt in full force, especially from the Room of Deviance. Mira's feet momentarily lost traction, slipping on gore that now covered large sections of the floor. Inside the DJ booth, a bot repeatedly slammed the head of the human DJ into the oversized control board, creating a staccato symphony of death, before the final head-slam broke through the casing, with an electric explosion that killed both the DJ and the music.

Horatio moved cautiously through the crowd, panic slowly building as he realized he was on the wrong side of what was quickly escalating into a massacre. He maintained a low profile, pushing through the crowd against the tide, until he could go no farther. Horatio found himself in a small bubble of space, in the middle of which stood Mira, face spattered with blood, but her piercing green eyes unmistakable. Or so he thought.

"Mira," he questioned out. The bot paused, eye meeting eye, then she quickly moved on. Springing onto the elderly patron he had been by moments before. Horatio forced himself to look away as the bot started to raise bloodied fist. *What the fuck is happening.* "Mira!"

Mira grabbed his shoulder, "Horatio, it's me!" He turned with a startle.

"God what happened to you?"

"Someone from the Center got me, he was taking me away when I touched another bot and suddenly she went berserk attacking him. I started touching as many as I could."

"This is it, this is our break!"

We can take this whole Temple tonight!" Their eyes met and, although his were no match in intensity, justice burned for both. Every spec of hope that had been stolen came back in a flood. And again, like that, was absorbed back into the abyss.

There was no time to react as an unstable bolt of energy smashed into the side of Mira's face, slamming her sideways off her feet. Horatio's face dropped, he turned in what felt like slow motion towards the direction of the bolt. Dozens of soldiers filed into the Temple, armed with energy cannons they fired indiscriminately through the crowd. The beam that reached Mira's face had left its trail of destruction in the form of human and robotic limbs littered amongst dropped bodies. Humans, and green-eyed robots sputtered out cries of anguish, the blue eyed ones only twitched. Horatio could hear the cannon-generator's whine climb in intensity, unable to move out of the way as two more beams indiscriminately cut swaths through the people who had been standing on either side of him.

Out of the chaos, Mira's hand appeared and clutched Horatio's coat, pulling him to the floor moments before another cannon unleashed its deadly payload. "Thanks," Horatio said breathlessly, only now noticing Mira's face. Half the faux flesh had been burnt away, exposing a metallic bone structure underneath. Her left eye was now filled only with green static, and the sight left him feeling ill and helpless.

"Stay down, we have to make our way back to the skywalk," the words barely made it out of Mira's mouth before an explosion detonated close enough to set Horatio's ears ringing. Keeping low they managed to progress only a few more feet, before a clank drew their attention. The tossed grenade left them no choice but to run as fast as possible. Mira took the brunt of the explosion, thrown into Horatio, and together they smashed through the weakened window behind them.

Wind whipped their clothes about as they fell. Horatio didn't respond to Mira's shouts. Mira stretched out. Air touched her fingers the first few swipes, as they continued their freefall. Floor after floor zipped by. Another desperate swipe. Relief flooded Mira as her fingertips clasped the sleeve of

Horatio's jacket. She held him close, and braced herself.

***

The Luminescent must have had forewarned the Temple Guard, they had already brought out the Spit Cannons as he reached their weapons storage. Though distant, Gustav could hear the distinct electric spit discharged by these fearsome weapons—4 clustered shots. Gustav grabbed his own weapon, a light but deadly dark-metaled quarterstaff. 3 clustered shots. Ignoring the occasional shock of a grenade, he ran down the short hall leading to the stairs, and his proximity released the lock. Another explosion rocked soot free from the stairs. As Gustav continued up, he heard only two additional shots followed by another detonation.

Gustav dropped to a knee as soon as the door opened, a blast sizzled the frame. The velocity of the round had been slowed passing through enough bodies on its trajectory to leave only a scorch mark. The scene Gustav watched unfold before his eyes vanquished any hope of an easy victory. One of the guards, attempting to block bots from reaching the elevators, had his arm ripped off with sheer brute force. The cannon fell from his grasp, and the attacking bot tossed away the useless appendage as casually as a piece of litter. In an instant three other bots descended to beat the fallen guard. The lobby had six more infected bots that watched, that smiled. The Vanguard had been completely decimated.

As the door clicked closed behind him, all jaded eyes turned on him. The lobby was demolished, and the lights flickered causing spurts of darkness. He stepped cautiously, one bot moved in similarity towards him. The bot was so damaged he could no longer tell the sex it had been designed for. He held its green eyes with his. Their mechanical movements disgusted him. Gustav lunged, a hard step forward with an extended arm that sent the end of the staff square into its chest. It blasted back with an electrical charge.

Two twisted their head in question, and watched as the other seven charged. Gustav met their exuberance, he jumped forward and brought his staff down on One. The head dented, and the bot skidded back. He let himself get surrounded. The butt of the staff moved low and out that easily swept a leg, the discharge on contact sent Two into a backwards flip. A quick thrust to his left, then to right sent Three and Four crashing into walls. Letting go of his two handed stance, he viciously swept around the air with one. The extended reach let him smash Five and Six in the face making their bodies crumple against a half burnt receptionist desk. Pulling back, he hard swung under his arm, just enough to graze Seven behind him. The discharge sent her back into the door he had come through.

He looked forward at the two left, the lights blinked out momentarily again. In that moment the two sets of green fire moved at him, one moved far right, the other held to his close left. The left set of eyes turned sideways as he thrusted out, the lights blinked back on. The bot had its feet dug into the

24

wall, her toes ripped in and out of the metal like butter as she ran along it. Gustav's perception slowed the events, he had just missed her and knew there was nothing he could do to stop the bot's next attack. It came swiftly, only two or three crouched steps along the wall before she reached an arm out around his neck. The full momentum of her attack brought Gustav to the floor with such force all air exited his lungs. He gasped for breath as her hand clamped onto his shoulder. Each finger forced itself into his body.

Gustav bellowed being dragged, he held the staff clumsily as he swung haphazardly over his head. He connected, the jolt blasted them apart, and in an instant cauterized the four finger holes in his shoulder. The lights flickered out again, he rolled to his back. He scanned the darkness feverishly, his breath held. Left. Right. Up. He caught the two emerald embers above him. The moment's hesitation was all he needed to aim and fire. The lobby illuminated as an electrical bolt jetted from the end of the staff, and almost instantly struck the bot. The mechanical body fell to Gustav's feet, the lights flicked on again.

The elevator chimed, Temple Cleaners spilled into the lobby. Gustav was back on his feet, finally able to take in the immense scale of the devastation. The doors that led to the Deviation Room had been completely reduced to a charred hole. Blood and oil smeared the walls and drenched the floors. The closest cleaner walked towards him wearing the standard white jumpsuit, but the oversized analytical goggles were his own. A ring of ginger hair that was only slightly bigger than the band that held goggles poked out. He smiled broadly.

"Gustav!" He said with an extended hand.

"Luminescent sent you?"

"It's me, Jerry!"

"I know."

With a nod Jerry's smile fell and he withdrew his hand. "Yes, the Luminescent notified us you were, uh, done, in here."

"A fast response time. They may have given the order a bit too soon." Gustav responded with an empty smile.

"Right, right," Jerry said resuming his smile and pointedly ignoring any subtext. "You know them, to a T some would say. Impressive work, anyway."

Gustav felt a bit guilty. Jerry was old-school in every respect, and Gustav had no desire to insult him. He simply wanted the night to be over.

"Thank you, you should find eight disabled but in fairly decent condition. I dented one pretty severely. The other was ruined before I arrived on the scene."

"Hm, great. Really fascinating, isn't it? I've never seen anything like this before. You?"

"No, never. Hopefully never again. Anyone significant make the casualty list?"

"No, I mean there was one minor politician, a few officers. But they'll be considered heroes elsewhere tonight. No better legacy than giving your life for the cause."

Gustav knew full well that Jerry's sentiments only extended to *others* dying for his cause. To be fair, Jerry's devotion to the Luminescent almost matched Gustav's own, but there is a distinct difference to be willing to lay your own life on the line, and being the one who cleaned up the messes afterward.

"You said it brother," Gustav said as he passed by to the elevators.

***

Mira and Horatio had taken refuge inside an abandoned sewer system, knowing full well they were living on borrowed time. It wouldn't be long before the cleaners determined she wasn't in the pile of parts left at the Temple. After minutes of quiet contemplation at the bottom, Horatio in her arms, she realized she could see him. It was as if she put on a high contrast black and white television. The abandoned sewer system had been left for so long that rust was the only indication water had ever been present. Horatio slumped onto her back as she hoisted him. They ventured further into the tunnel.

The relative calm after the storm, provided space for Mira's thoughts to roam freely. She lingered on a memory of a moment spent with her parents. Then her thoughts fast-forwarded to the last moments of her life with stunning clarity. She could feel the barrel of the gun against her back, and her newly-expanded knowledge informed her it was a .50 caliber revolver digging into her left shoulder blade. She recalled the frigid metal cuffs that wrapped around her wrists.

Lao, Neikia, Gwendolynn, and Jason stood in a line cuffed as well. She was forced to observe their fate through a narrow glass window in the box-car in which she was confined. Five soldiers held them at gunpoint, masks covered their faces. The soldiers readied their HPB Rifles. The scene paused, Mira stood still, before allowing her memory reel to continue. She now noticed details that had escaped her attention in the actual moment. Gwendolynn's solitary tear. Lao's clenched jaw. The images held a second longer, before fire erupted from all five rifles. A red mist lingered in the air after the bodies of her teammates fell. It dissipated with the memory.

Revulsion coursed through Mira's artificial veins. She concentrated, replayed the thought to recollect something about her attackers and how they could have discovered their infiltration plan. Anger touched her as she remembered foolishly looking at the handwritten note underneath the window slit. The gun went against her at that moment. The card fell before she opened it to read. Forced to watch her family murdered again. A moment after, the hammer fell. The large caliber obliterated her heart, tore open her chest. Darkness, then Horatio. She replayed her death, looked at Horatio.

It was Mira who was responsible for the decision to leave Horatio behind to detonate the bomb, both knowing she was sending him on suicide mission, and it was more difficult than ever to shake off her feelings of guilt. His volunteerism replayed incessantly, an instinctive defense mechanism. Her guilt forced another memory to play, the moment she found him after Catherine's death. Now she was paying the ultimate karmic price for sentencing a teammate to death, her own deathless death. She could only take solace in the hope that somehow her, and Horatio's "rebirth" would allow them a second chance to uncover mystery that motivated their original insurrection but, for the time being, the mysteries only seemed to be multiplying in number.

Was her brain on ice somewhere, her head hollowed out, connected to a server? Possible scenarios for her current predicament swirled through Mira's consciousness. Suddenly, she was struck by an equally unthinkable notion. Was Horatio real? She touched a hand against his face, the still-wet blood stuck to her hand. There was no taste, only a sudden knowledge of its composition, proteins and water, blood. Frustrated at her own lack of faith her hand jutted out, the sewer's side gave way easily. She cautiously peered over as she cleared a path to the other side. Through her one remaining good eye, an expanse of columns greeted her cyclopean sight.

She had heard tales about the old system of carts, but she never paid them much attention. People had always been sedentary, and it was difficult to imagine them any other way. The amount of work necessary to create this future, however, contradicted that appraisal. It was a grim thought that all this former industrious served only to create a future that allowed the population to remain cocooned in the Temple, interacting with the leaders strictly through a screen.

She walked forward absorbed by the complex system spread out before her. She had momentarily forgotten Horatio's presence, until a barely audible grunt brought her attention back to him. She knelt down and helped him lean against a column. She searched around for something to bandage his wounds, and a door caught her attention. The latch was secured, but a forceful downturn from her powerful arm and the entire handle broke free, finally she was able to enter.

The small bathroom contained only a broken a mirror, and a porcelain sink. Someone had long ago absconded with the toilet. She moved in closer to the mirror, resting her hands on the sink to steady herself. What she saw was a stark black-and-white vision of what she had become, unrecognizable to herself. Her damaged eye hung lifeless, dangling over her exposed metallic jaw. She painlessly popped it back into the ruined socket, bringing it back to life slowly. *What have they done to me? Am I even me?* She felt a sense of heat smoldering throughout her body. It was the first time she had felt anything since awakening inside the egg.

She welcomed the surge of anger coursing through her. It felt good. Without even realizing it, she had already ripped the sink off the wall, clutching at the porcelain with such intensity the edges turned to dust. The remnants of the crumbled sink fell to her feet. A new thought entered her consciousness, an all-consuming unshakeable notion. *I can be the monster. I can be what the Council fears!* The thought ran fever-like through her brain. She stared into the mirror, into her own robotic eyes.

Mira's fist shattered what remained of the mirror, forming a new network of cracks on the wall behind it. Her other fist followed suit. Again. Over and over. Her fury against the wall shredded the

30

artificial skin covering her hands. Her metal palms slammed against it. The room rumbled. Faux flesh ripped away as her fingers dug into the concrete. Chunks of stone torn loose, rebar pried out and tossed aside. Sparks spat from her broken phalanges. She only balled up her remaining ones and struck out, pounding over and over, until all that remained of her hands was mangled machinery. Mira still didn't relent as she threw them into the wall, expending all of her anger, her hate.

Illumination extended, a spiraled beam of energy vaporized the wall. It left a field of destruction through two more columns, the entire station shook. Mira stepped through her recently created hole in amazement. She stared at her wrists only for a moment before throwing out her left arm, the expanse of trains and columns illuminated. Charged light flew out, a cloud of dust tailed it. The sound came moments after the energy beam ripped through space. Destruction flared out in the wake, blowing her ponytailed hair back with the aftershock. She held her handless arms in front of her face again. Sparks spat, and illuminated her space. An almost maniacal grin spread over her ruined face. *I'll bring their world down to me. I'll bring them all down to me!*

She moved her arms to her right side, and she concentrated her mind. Focused on what she wanted, held it until she felt it to her core. For the first time, with absolute certainty, she knew there was no need for anyone's help to bring down the Luminescent. She felt all-powerful. "I'll murder them all," Mira roared, throwing her arms out.

Unstable jets of energy soared in a blinding streak. Matter caught in its path ripped apart or vaporized. Instant illumination, followed by impenetrable nothingness. A stillness that lasted only a second, before the unsupported roads suddenly began to give way. The street rumbled, windows blew out of the Temple above, the entrance began to crumble. A sinkhole of sorts began to form and grow, indiscriminately pulling in streets, homeless, and vehicles, growing until its wake of destruction reached the edges of another Temple. Mira noticed with surprise that she and Horatio had only made it a few blocks in their escape.

Mira hopped easily into the center of the newly-created hole that linked the station to the city. Above her neon lights bathed everything in their garish glow. It disgusted her. She looked about her, the signs boldly declared what they had always declared. She stood dwarfed by the temple, bathed in the non-stop neon colors of the city. Consume, fuck, destroy, consume, fuck, destroy, consume, fuck, destroy. She instantly decided to follow their advice.

Mira jumped up high, her arms stretched out. A powerful beam of energy struck against the building. Throwing her arms down to her sides, she blasted two additional columns of light into the ground, opening the hole even wider as Mira's body propelled upward in a burst. The momentary sense of weightlessness surged through her like a trance-inducing drug. She punched out, a chunk of energy hurtled towards the building. Another powerful blast spouted. Another. Another. Mira continued her onslaught until half of the Temple's façade was vaporized or caved in. Joy overrode her senses. Intoxicated with power she fell back down to earth, spinning and twisting as she indiscriminately baptized the city with the water of her hatred.

Chapter 3
Power and Control

It was chaos in the truest sense of the word. Gustav could only speculate how many bots were turned in this wave. Fire continued to rage around the sinkhole that had engulfed half of the Temple. What Gustav found even more inexplicable was the random pattern of holes that had been pocketed throughout the building with such destructive force.

Gustav called out orders to his men from the passenger seat of the security vehicle, "Go straight in Frie, they'll be coming hard at us, but just use your staffs."

Frie sped the car through the landscape of desolation. Wrecked vehicles, and fires everywhere, but not a single bot or living person to be seen. "The street-lifers must have all run off. Let's approach the edge of the sinkhole."

"Sir, no contacts."

"It would appear so Misant," Gustav said absently. The car pulled to a stop, and he motioned for Misant, and Frie to stay. "Janic, on me. Stay Close."

The two exited the car with caution, both held their staffs in a white-knuckled grip. They edged to the sinkhole, smoke obstructed their view for a moment.

Mira stood amidst the rubble. A poshly-suited man lying stomach down clutched her foot on the side of his face in a silent plea. She showed no sign of remorse as she brought her foot down holding just before his skull cracked. He screamed as he bent his arms to desperately grab and punch at her leg. In an instant she brought her foot down the rest of the way, a pop of blood erupted under her sole.

Mira turned her head. Ponytail gone, her hair scattered in the wind. She turned her unmistakable green eyes in Gustav's direction. Without hesitation, she threw out her left arm. A pulse of plasma careened towards Gustav, and his companion. The seasoned leader instinctively threw himself to the ground. Beside him Janic's waist smoldered, her legs twitched. He couldn't pull his eyes from this horrific sight, even as he twisted his own body and moved back into the car. He felt he was still staring as he barked out orders. "Go! Backwards, go now go!"

The picture was frozen over his eyes. He didn't see her jump out of the hole. He didn't see her extend. Only burnt flesh and smoke filled his mind. Gustav had to force himself to look at reality, he grabbed at the wheel and wrenched the car sharply to the right, but not in time. The shot vaporized the engine, and front left tire. Glass shattered, the car spun. They came to a crashing to a halt against another wrecked car.

"Captain, oh God captain!"

Gustav labored to clear his double-vision. "Frie, what's wrong?" All he heard in response was ragged breathing. "Frie?"

Gustav finally managed to turn his head to survey the damage. Most of the front left of the car was gone. Frie's knee and elbow extended at unnatural angles, smoking in the exposed air, the wounds were cauterized.

"Ca... Ca..." Frie sputtered out. His body shook violently.

Gustav's comm came to life. "Captain Recht. This is Luminescent. We don't have time to explain, but there's a copter in-bound to you with Carthy, and Pierce. You can save the second lieutenant's life, however he must submit to the bot program."

Gustav looked around. "This is Luminescent?"

"Do you not hear the copter?"

Gustav listened and could hear it in the distance in the gaps between explosive discharges. For the moment, Mira appeared to have lost interest in them. Mere flies to swat, and forget? Gustav went to question again, but was cut off. He busied himself by injecting Frie with a shot of adrenaline.

"Second Lieutenant Frie, if you wish to live, you must tell us you submit to The Program. You will be installed with an overdrive, but you will not lose your identity or your consciousness. It's your only chance for survival."

Frie looked to Gustav, his short breaths slowly coming under control.

"This is all you Frie, I'll respect whatever choice you make." Tears fell from Frie as he nodded.

"We need you to affirmatively answer." Were they watching? Gustav looked to Frie, he could see the spit fly as he cried out in affirmation. A ripped yes.

"Pierce has landed the copter half a mile west of you. Carthy will walk you through the procedure. Take point Captain Recht."

Gustav climbed through the window of the wrecked vehicle, and made his way unsteadily to his

36

feet. He feared the sinkhole would continue to grow if that bot continued to fire into the Temple. With a single swipe of his combat knife, Gustav released Frie from the restraining seat belt, and hefted his comrade's body over his shoulder for the long trek to the copter through the smoldering ruins. The second lieutenant fell onto the cold copter floor as Gustav threw him off his shoulder.

"My god," murmured Carthy. "A bot did this?"

"How the fuck do we save him!"

The words silenced the rest of the team. This was the first time they had heard their Captain swear. "Overdrive," Carthy said handing Gustav what looked like an electronic ice pick, green goo filled the middle. "Jam this into his brain, twist handle, snap off."

Gustav handled the drive. He had seen chartreuse colored liquid before. "Frie?"

"Please," he whimpered through gritted teeth.

Gustav grabbed him by his collar. He withdrew his knife, and placed the hilt between Frie's teeth. Turning him over, Gustav took a single deep breath. He brought the drive straight down into the back of his comrade's head. The scream overpowered the electric explosions, a scream that pierced the heart of even the most battle-hardened among them. A few moments, and Frie went silent. Another moment, tremors overtook his body. After another few slipped by his body calmed, he opened his eyes and sat up.

"Kid? You good?"

Frie looked at Gustav, he stared a moment before hugging his captain with his one good arm, unsuccessfully fighting tears. He felt awkward, on the verge of pushing him off. Instead he allowed the moment. Misant whispered to Pierce, "bot's don't cry. That's all the proof I need."

Gustav couldn't help but have reservations about the choice his second lieutenant had made, as he noted the tears of relief that flooded Fries' eyes. The rest of the squad piled into the copter, and Gustav pulled himself up with a grunt. They lifted into the air. Below they could see Luminescent vehicles erupt in flames. Gustav surveyed what remained of the city. How much would be standing by the time this all ended? Irritation held him as they flew away from the battlefield.

***

The destroyed entrance of the Temple gaped open, yet there were still those who attempted to escape through the rear. Mira laughed maniacally at the sight of the bots who tried to soothe the fleeing hordes. Some, broken, moved in spurts as they tried to coerce fleeing victims into having sex. Sparks of electricity shocked the people they reached out to. Men and women, young and old, all humans tried desperately to escape with their lives.

Every inch of the temple Mira brought down fueled her euphoria, she needed another inch, another body, another... suddenly her vision rippled. Her remaining good eye focused automatically on a suit trying to escape. *A Luminescent! One of them is actually here!"* Giddy with anticipation, she threw a smaller bolt of energy just under him. The ground ruptured beneath him, flinging him and a few others up against the wall before they toppled down into the newly created crater. Mira hopped twenty feet towards the suit, another thirty feet, grabbed him by the lapel, and looked into his eyes. The fear on his face was euphoric, she threw his body back to the center of the hole with a sickening crack. The sound brought a dark smile to Mira's lips.

Gravity felt non-existent as she leapt again after him, she wasn't yet finished. The suit whimpered, desperately trying to crawl from her reach. Mira took her time approaching him, savoring the moment. She placed her foot firmly on his head, and slowly applied pressure. This was her new instrument, she would trumpet her justice with a crescendo of their screams. His pitch climbed, as she met the limit of his skulls resistance. With an upsurge of power, her foot came down hard. The sloppy pop satisfied her soul. She turned to look at the two watching. *That insufferable agent. Not this time!*

The blast annihilated one of them. Mira threw her head back with a laugh, shaking the hair out of her face, and leapt towards them. The car screeched as it sped back. *Too late,* she thought with an out thrown hand. The car lit up. Satisfaction washed over her face as she moved both of her arms out to the side, washing the buildings and streets in her light. The destruction roared. More vehicles approached. Three vans. She swatted two away with bolts that incinerated them at the midsection. They smoked, and veered into a collision path. Mira threw out both arms at the last one. *A grand finale.* Nothing. She threw them out again. As panic set in, so did her awareness of a faint beeping sound that had previously escaped her attention. Now it was a drum, a slow funeral dirge. The van struck her full force, throwing her back into the very hole she had created.

The box-shaped van swerved in an attempt to stop, but its weight and momentum rolled it into the hole as well. Mira struggled to a standing position, a few hundred feet away from her attackers. She clung for support to half-standing column. Mira tried to run but tripped over her feet. It was as though she was moving through water. Each step required calculation and precision, lest she risk another fall. Her progress was painfully slow. A figure blasted out the window of the van, and Mira could hear someone running towards her from the distance. She turned slowly, ready to accept her fate head-on. Her assailant, wearing full body armor, stood on a mound of rubble, raised his shotgun, and pulled the trigger. The gun jerked, and the shot went wide. Horatio's arms were locked around the soldier as they both fell down the mound of rubble.

The two men hit hard, grappling amidst the rubble for control of the weapon. Horatio grabbed the trooper by his vest with both hands, it summoned an automatic response. The head-butt knocked Horatio back to the ground momentarily senseless. The trooper made a dash for the shotgun, gripping it, and twisting around towards Horatio. Horatio held the pin in the air, He twisted his back to the explosion. A pink mist lingered momentarily in the still air.

Horatio laid on the ground, his ears ringing, He motioned for Mira to keep going. She agreed with his silent command, and her pace increased as she concentrated her energy entirely on her legs. However, the increase energy usage caused the other systems to shut down. Her eye once static, was now dead completely, hearing reduced. Mira limped forward, and moved with some speed down the corridor. Night vision gone. She continued, further and further into the dark. A light, a couple of lights. Mira ducked down in slow motion, her back against a train. Horatio startled her as he touched her shoulder. She sat down, arms going limp to her side. "You have to run, start a new group, be the new Mutinist. Please, don't let our work die here," Mira words came out scrambled, the distortion rang with self-conscious mockery into her heart.

"The explosion was this way," one of the troopers yelled out. Three torch beams sweeping the area, heading in their direction. Their discovery was imminent.

"Stay here," Horatio said, realizing the unintended irony only afterwards. He crouched low to the ground, moving as quickly as he could towards the van.

"There! There's one of them, fire!"

Bullets pinged off the rubble he had just dropped behind, a clear path to the van laid before him. Horatio ran, pain evaporating with a new surge of adrenaline. He knew he had only one chance. Horatio plunged through the broken window. Shards of glass tore jagged holes through his pants, and gnawed at his knees as he crawled inside.

Mira moved as close against the column as she could. They rushed by, she followed slowly. She reached the mound as they entered the clearing. A barrage of bullets cut through the side of the van.

Horatio caught two in the storm of magnetic propelled bullets, their body rattled as their armor withstood the first few hits. In less than a second spurts of blood peppered their bodies. The one who rolled out of the way laid prone, drawing her side arm she began taking shots at the van.

By the time she had gotten off her ninth shot, Mira had finally made it behind her. She had a piece of rebar gripped tightly. Every fitful step brought her closer to the last remaining soldier. Unable to even lift her makeshift weapon, Mira simply allowed herself to fall, pinning the trooper to the ground like an insect specimen. With a guttural gasp the soldier began to struggle, twisting their arm awkwardly to shoot behind them. One of the remaining three shots grazed off Mira's metal shoulder. Mira fell forward, her head against the soldier's shoulder. She breathed in and out, focused on her scent receptors. *Does death have a scent?* The pinned soldier continued to spurt, and grunt with a few final twitches before expiring.

Mira managed to muster enough energy to croak out, "Horatio." Her voice sounded even more robotic than before.

The digitized call was a far cry from her voice, but Horatio held to the belief that it was Mira. The real Mira. He sat there for a moment, still holding the spent HPB rifle. The smoke from the gun had filled the van in a soft haze. It made him feel as if he were in a dream. That this was his death visage, none of it real. However, the pain he felt when he finally tried to crawl out of the van brought him back to reality with crystal clarity. He touched the side of his leg, and his fingers brought back blood.

Extricated from the wreckage of the van, Mira greeted him. She held a small can in her hand.

"Horatio," she said in slow motion, taking a knee to lower herself to his level as he laid in the rubble. The Temple continued to blaze above them. He sat up with great pain, his pants drenched in blood. He ripped them open, and Mira immediately sprayed his wound. An involuntary squeak of pain escaped Horatio, his wound seared with new agony. There was always this level of intense pain when the nanobots did their work, welding the flesh back together from the inside-out. "Are you able to stand?"

Horatio finally got his first good look at Mira's completely altered visage from just a few hours earlier. Blood and oil caked what was left of her face. The stumps where he hands had formerly been still emitted an occasional spark. Her dress, drenched with more blood than pink fabric, was ripped and singed. But her one still-operational green eye pulled him back into its vortex. "Yes," he answered. With her assistance he made it to his feet.

They wandered together through the darkness, neither able to see much in front of them. The abandoned tracks kept them on a path that led them inexorably forward. The silence broken every few minutes by the beep of Mira's energy alarm. With each beep, Horatio's mind returned to the moment he found her inside the egg-pod. He should have been the one to have died. He would gladly exchange places with her. Mira's wrist on his arm stopped him. He felt a battery-like jolt.

43

When they came to a standstill, Horatio could hear the grunts that prompted Mira's caution, and they both slowly stepped backwards acting out of pure instinct. A beaten bot fell to the floor right where they had been standing, and the light from his collar illuminated the area in a soft blue hue.

Further ahead of them, a man stepped out from in front of an abandoned train. It was clear he was unaware of their presence. "You stupid bitch, you're just a dirty whore." He laughed, and saddled the bot. His badge glimmered in the light. He was a member of the Luminescent Guard.

Horatio and Mira stood transfixed in shock and horror as they watched the scene being played out in front of them.

"Cry. Be afraid," the Guard said, touching his wrist to the bot's waist. The bot immediately began to cry, desperately trying to push him away. The Guard struck the bot across the face with his fist before grabbing it in his grimy hands. He continued to laugh as he struck the disabled bot again, as hard as he could. The face of the bot tore open, revealing its metallic understructure. "You dumb fucking bitch," he yelled in the bot's ruined face. The guard gripped the bot's throat, strained and grunted, until the bot became completely silent. The silence broke with a beep from Mira's warning sensor.

The guard immediately reached for his gun, Horatio collided against him. Both fell hard against the cement floor of the station, knocking the gun out of reach. The officer instinctively pulled his knife, and with one quick move dug it deeply into Horatio's shoulder. Mira could only watch, limping slowly towards her endangered friend. She no

44

longer had the energy to even speak, words shouted in her head she could not vocalize. She willed out her hand, the last of her energy. Mira fell to a knee, then completely flat on her face. Her consciousness drifted.

Horatio held his shoulder, and screamed as he tried to pull the knife. He finally ripped it out with an accompanying spurt of blood. An indication that the knife had slashed a major artery. "Oh God," he moaned trying to stem the flow of blood from his wound. The officer, gun in hand, took aim. A gunshot resounded. Horatio watched the officer fall. Blood oozed out between his fingers as he tried to look for his savior. Black dots obstructed his view, he fell into unconsciousness.

Chapter 4
Rather Than Love, Money, Fame

"Welcome to Verite."

"Where's my friend," Horatio asked.

"Relax, we're here to help."

"That's why I'm tied up?" Horatio laid strapped to a medical table. The ten by ten room looked clean and sleek. The only thoughts that occupied his head were that the Luminescent had surely captured him. He twisted his wrists around, checked the tightness of his restraints.

"For our safety, of course. You and your... friend have been through quite the trauma. You could've woke up attacking. But let me reassure you, we are here to help."

"O.k. I have no reason to argue. So, help."

The man's lab coat matched his light blue eyes, worn. His smile, on the other hand, seemed fresh and genuine. "Je ne se qua," he said undoing Horatio's bonds.

"I don't know what," Horatio murmured, rubbing his wrists. "That's the original call. How do you know that? Where am I?"

"I told you, Verite. My name is Frederick." His lab coat opened as he moved to a table with a sink to reveal a worn white collared shirt, and faded grey slacks. "Where your Mutinist was the body of the resistance, we would, humbly mind you, call ourselves the brain. We hide here, gathering and storing knowledge. Looking for that smoking gun of truth." He had poured a glass of water in the midst of his speech.

"The truth of what we don't know. How serendipitous," Horatio said with a cut. He looked to his coat that hung on the chair, it'd been cleaned and patched. Moving to towards it he shrugged it on gingerly. Every movement sent small sparks of pain across his body.

Frederick had moved silently, and was in his face as he turned, the glass held out. "Incredulous, aren't we?"

"I would hope you would be too, if you were really with the resistance." He took the water, drank the full glass, and handed it back. His thirst had won out over his suspicion. Leaning against the wall his eyes took in the utensils and equipment. Small sticks of metal, bladed instruments, and mechanical maintenance tools.

"You, and the Mutinist are all that's left of your faction. If there was ever a time for leaps of faith, now would be it." Frederick set the glass down, and half sat against the counter.

"Some would say the exact opposite," Horatio retorted.

"As I was saying, we are the brain. Your group did the hard work. The work that helps now. Every break we've received has been from the Mutinist, and her team."

Horatio held his head. It throbbed. "Where is my... where is my bot."

"You'd refer to the Mutinist as a bot?" Now it was the man's turn to be in disbelief.

Horatio's eyes shot up to meet his. He stared. *How could he possibly know that?* "Take me to her."

Frederick smiled, and walked to the door. He opened it, and waited for Horatio to walk through.

***

"Hey kid."

"Captain," Frie replied, his face a portrait of listlessness.

"How you feeling," Gustav asked, taking a seat bedside.

Silence greeted him. His metallic arm was supposed to be at the elbow, where he had lost. The Luminescent must have disagreed. It was sleek though, and merged perfectly into his skin at the shoulder.

"How's that mech feel? Pretty impressive."

Again silence.

"You'll be back in the fray before you know it."

"I want to go back in now," Frie said as he finally turned to look his captain in the eyes.

"Well..."

"I've spoken with the doctors, I'm ready now."

Gustav rested his stare on the empty bed across from him. "Your body may be. Your arm and leg might be. But is your mind? Could you possibly keep your head in the game right now?"

Frie resumed his silence.

"Captain. We have intel on an imminent attack. It's the Mutinist."

Gustav, and Frie met eyes once more. The sudden noise from Gustav's comm startled both. "My mistake, I thought I turned off my communicator." Frie's face pleaded. "No."

The lieutenant looked away. "Feel well soon Frie," Gustav said. He rested a hand of reassurance on his partner's new mechanized shoulder. Gustav's heart anchored him as he stepped towards the door. A Hesitation that halted him, and gave Frie a small sense of hope. Only a moment, then the door opened, and clicked closed behind him.

Gustav moved swiftly down the hall, he touched his earpiece, he wanted a private conversation. "Luminescent." A moment. Another moment.

"Gustav." A gruff voice greeted him on the line. He instantly recognized it as Bernard's.

"My heart, and soul Luminescent." Even when they couldn't see him, he still raised his fist to his heart. Even when he hated them.

"Is there something wrong Gustav?" It was Janice.

Gustav could only decipher the names through monotonous study of all archived announcements any Luminescent had ever given. The six members, the council that ran their concrete forest, held very few. Though to be fair, they were more decrees than announcements. New steps, and innovations for the society at large. Temple installation was the very first one. The granting of sidewalks another. The ban on modification came fifty years ago, after a rogue cyborg attack. Control of all bots then shifted to the Council of Luminescence.

"How did you access my communications device?" Straightforward, they were on the same team, so no need for subterfuge. Gustav knew his comm device was off.

"According to the Leverage Act, instituted when we took our seats, we may access all dormant devices at times of crises. As later added by the Renegade Act: Synthetic, or organic dormant devices may be accessed at any time in situations dealing with robot security. Do you have an issue with us utilizing our legislative right?" The stuffy voice that droned belonged to Mathis, a weathered man that only spoke on matters of legality.

"No, however I was bedside with Lieutenant Frie."

"Is he accompanying you," Janice resumed control, a static garble interrupted her speech.

"No. Absolutely not."

"Mm, why," Bernard drawled.

"He's not well enough."

"Bots are able to work immediately," he pressed.

"He's not a bot." Heat covered Gustav's words.

"I see no reason for a discussion on humanities," Mathis interrupted, "You will take Lieutenant Frie to deal with the Mutinist."

"I'm afraid so, a fire with fire situation." Bernard interjected, "Unless, you yourself wish to submit to the bot program. You could single handedly police the entire district."

Janice cut in quickly, "Yes. Your strength and aptitude. I dare say he could even challenge us."

Gustav had reached his car by now, sitting in the quiet interior his head ran a million miles. "I do not wish to seem ungrateful, but I could never undergo such an option."

"Is there something wrong with being a bot," Kristoff intruded. Were his words snide?

"My humanity is my everything. I have no need for..."

"Very well. However, taking Frie is an order. Are you aware the Mutinist killed Jeffrey?" Matilda spoke now, head of the council, the Valkyrie of Scelus. Her words were covered in ice.

"Uh, no I had no idea." Gustav's speech stumbled, he hated himself. She always made his throat clench.

"Gather your team at Processing Center Four in an hour."

Gustav sat in his car for a moment. Touched his comm, "Team." He looked at his watch, it indicated everyone was connected. "PC four, one hour." He touched his comm again. Silence now lingered in the air, it calmed him to some extent. Lights came alive on the dashboard as he started the engine. They bathed him in a neon blue hue. The drive was quick, centralized living quarters for all Luminescent personal. A building of intimidation, bathed in a pristine ghost white color. Home to the virtuous.

A beep chirped from his wristwatch as his door unlocked. Gustav's apartment greeted him with the comforts of his personality. An ebony piano was displayed prominently in the living room. It called to him. He let his fingers touch over a set of keys that filled his soul with sorrow. He found beauty in sadness, and in particular sorrowful tunes. He twisted himself slightly to see his clock, five thirty. He touched out an awkward tune, a small door in the front of the piano opened up. He took out a small round silicone container, popped the top. He licked his finger, dipped it in, then touched five

51

large crystals onto his tongue. He preferred his own dosage to the preset. Cap on, container replaced, another few keyes. It shut with a click.

He played an actual song now. Slow deliberate keys that cried out in his silent apartment. The last note died out. Again he enjoyed the silence. Rising, he went to the kitchen for a large glass of water, then went to his closet. He swallowed a large gulp as he pondered removing his trophy revolver still stained with blood. *It would do nothing, though if I could kill 7 with it... no the team will eliminate him easy enough. I must focus on the Mutinist. How many times must I corner her!* His thoughts rose fires in his mind. Finishing the water he turned his gaze to the Eel Rifle that hung by its strap on a coat hanger. Setting the glass on the shelf he reached for it, handling it with familiarity. He aimed down the scope, checked the charge, then shouldered the weapon.

***

Verite was a far cry from the laboratory Horatio had just exited. A repurposed deep station with three levels. He found himself on a metal walkway of the second level, suspended over an all-encompassing park draped in holiday lights. Abandoned shops of the station where now reading rooms, libraries, stores, and cafes. A few still laid bare waiting for a purpose. It boggled Horatio's mind how many people were living free of Luminescent control.

The walkway clanged loudly as he stepped. Frederick was well ahead of him already. The faster steps shook the railway, and caused Frederick to steady himself with the handrail. He looked to Horatio who had caught up.

"How is this possible?"

"What do you mean?"

"Are you stealing everything to run this city?" The question felt rude after he blurted it out.

Frederick took it in stride, and laughed. "No of course not. We grow our own food, cobbled together EM Harvesters, and purify sewage water. We sustain ourselves."

"What if the Luminescent finds you?"

"They have," Frederick said, his tone turning somber. "There's been many Verites." The answer struck him as odd. Mira had never mentioned anything of the sort. Though to be honest he hadn't taken much stock in what seemed to be a mythical city. The debate of some resistance city always broke the monotony of their travels to and from missions. Catherine, and Lao were the only two true believes. Mira never spoke on the subject. Only that she funneled the info one-sidedly. Before Horatio could prod further Frederick came to a door. He knocked.

"Come in." The response flooded Horatio with relief. Frederick looked with a smile. He opened the door, and motioned for Horatio to go first. The room was almost in uniformity with the one they had left. His captain leaned against a wall cross armed.

Mira's face was repaired, her hair back to its normal brunette. Back to her messy bob, and side swept bangs. It appeared too that her voice was her own, back to stern ice. For all intents and purposes, she was Mira. A deadlier Mira, but her, nonetheless. Somehow they had found a green coat that matched her old yesteryear military style. It hung open and to her knees, a black shirt and jeans peeked from underneath.

Horatio wanted to hug her, though they had been side by side, he had on some level been hung up on her appearance. They had changed her into the flagship-bot. Millions had been produced over the last fifty years. Now it felt as if his leader had been retrieved from the jaws of hell. Like time had rewound to a week ago.

Frederick cleared his throat, and moved his arms in boisterous fashion, "as you know fifty years ago."

"Skip the history lesson Frederick. Just cut to it." And as a week ago, Mira's cold apathetic approach came back. Horatio looked at her, the last visages of doubt had evaporated.

"Well," Frederick smiled, "I wasn't looking for you. I was tracking the Luminescent you killed. We had a theory. And actually quite an elaborate plan. First we were to track him to the temple, infiltrate through a series of tunnels," Frederick then mumbled something about her destruction under his breath, "then use this little..." His smile faded at being cut off.

"Please, the point?"

Horatio shot her another look.

"Yes, well have you ever heard of an overdrive?"

"No," Mira cut off eye contact, perhaps the history lesson had been important. She didn't need to breath but took one to steady herself. The power coursed through her for action, it was almost rapacious to sit still and talk.

"Well to 'cut to the chase' let's just say it's the center of connection. It transmits everything to the Luminescent. Likewise they receive information. So much so that they utilize the most advanced nanobots in production. In fact, much of our research is focused on these nanobots. They're impossible to destroy."

"Even destroying the overdrive?" Horatio bruted his question in.

"Well therein lies the rub. According to our research, the nanobots completely disintegrate the overdrive. They in essence become the overdrive. An ever moving liquid device. Always transmitting, always receiving."

Now Mira interrupted, "And me? Am I transmitting?"

"No. As far as we know. You do not have any nanobots. Actually it was quite exciting, we had theories the inhibitors were within the nanobots. You seem to be... right my apologies." Mira's ostentatious look halted the analogy. Frederick tried to hurry his words. "You have an overdrive, but we have no idea how you are powered. The overdrive only allows your brain to interface with your mechanical body, but you still need energy. Nanobots, though able, can't pull in enough electromagnetic energy from the air to sustain what you did."

"Is that all that's left of me? My brain?"

The silence pierced Mira.

"Well there may be something else," Frederick piped up at last in hopeful protest. "As I said, it would be impossible for your brain alone to power the amount of destruction you caused. Whatever is powering you, it's incredible."

"Interesting, no?" The door clicked closed behind the words. Her insertion in their space, as well as their conversation was tranquil and flawless. Frederick placed his hand over his heart in salute.

"Allow me to introduce you to the other half of this operation, Olympe."

"Pleasure," She said with a playful curtsy. Her head tilted down and to the left with a smile which revealed her mechanical right eye. The pupil was a tapestry of metallic pastel colors that shimmered as it swirled. Her blonde hair, dirtied and frizzed, fell about her shoulders. Her lab coat spread opened in her curtsy revealed a dirtied shoulder strapped white dress. The frayed hem touched her shins.

"Olympe," Mira said with surprise. She continued at the bequest of a raised eyebrow. "I'm sorry, you are not what I expected."

"Almost think you expected me to be in diamonds," Olympe said with an upturned mouth.

Can bots blush, Mira thought to herself. In all honesty she did expect her to look queen like, the elegance with which she spoke always inclined her to think so. Through their seldom conversations she had heard regality drip off every word. Sharp, clear, and always a step ahead. "Expectation, Expectation, living my life at your dictation." An old nursery rhyme was all she could muster in response.

Olympe covered her mouth as she laughed, her other hand quickly extended for introductions. "It truly is a pleasure to meet both of you. Thank you for everything you've done Mira and Horatio. And that's for the past. Do you understand what we are on the verge of?"

"Pleasure as well. Frederick was about to inform us, until we became uh a little sidetracked," Horatio said as he shook her hand.

"Right well let me roll it out for you. Overdrive, mechanical body, and nanobots equals our traditional bots. We, ourselves, were able to create a smaller simulated overdrive to use mechanical parts such as my eye. We suspected the Luminescent were doing something similar to enhance the elite while everyone else was held back by the modification restriction."

"Suspected," Mira questioned.

Frederick smiled, "Now we know." He held up a small see-through bag, the overdrive still had bits of brain and blood spattered about it.

"Why's it intact," she pressed.

"Like I she said, nanobots. They're definitely being controlled whether to liquidate the mind or not. They still transmit, and receive. Still have inhibitors."

"So he was controlled," Horatio asked.

Frederick nodded. Olympe stepped in, "Well we can't say entirely controlled. I suspect whoever controls the bots has selective control over the Luminescent. Or anyone with these overdrives."

"Including me?"

"Ah-ha, that's where you are different. No nanobots. No inhibitors, no transmission. We have no clue what is powering you."

"What's powering you?" She shot back. Irritation gripped her with an undercurrent of trepidation.

"Captain!" Mira shot Horatio a look as he blurted out, it quelled him.

Olympe opened her right palm, a small illuminated circle laid in the middle. "A mixture. My battery uses air as an oxidizer, and connects to my heart and brain through gold nanowires. More than enough energy to power an eye."

"And you don't know what's powering me?"

"I have my suspicions, but it would be ridiculous to say at this stage." Mira began to protest, but was stopped with a raised hand. "Please, rest. We still need to do analysis of the overdrive. I believe there's valuable information to be retrieved. Let us work while you rest. I will have news for you shortly."

Mira, and Horatio left the small laboratory. Verite laid before them, rustic and aged. Carved out of the deep stations of yesteryear. People moved about, some laughing, some serious. The cafe across the gap of the second floor was the fourth Horatio had seen since he had woken. People read as if it were a casual undertaking. Horatio grabbed the railing, leaned against it until it began to groan. He stepped back cautiously.

"Can you believe it?"

"I knew it existed," Mira hesitated her eyes drinking in the vitality of the resistance, "Well no I guess I can't say that. I had hoped, and in a way that made it truly nonexistent to me. But even in those wildest fantasies, I didn't expect this."

Frederick joined them after a moment. "Horatio, I need you to make your way to the lower level. Look for a Horace, he'll set you up with everything you need. Mira, if you wouldn't mind coming this way?" The group parted ways. Frederick and Mira ascended the stairs as Horatio made his way down.

Chapter 5
Our Hubris

Further, and further down Horatio trudged. He felt burnt out, hounded to the edges of insanity. His fingers touched over the corroded bars of the stairs. He stopped, gripped the rail, and tugged. His mind was known to tease him, and he would frequently ground himself. Balled fist rubbed his eyes, and he continued on. The air felt heavy, and warm. He took a deep breath, what was that scent? His trudge picked up pace. The bottom of the stairs were damp. It was almost dark where he stood, a light shined underneath the door in front of him.

The entry gave way to a brilliance that forced him to cover his eyes. His nostrils were stormed by the petrichor in the air. It's earthy aroma instantly seduced him, and threatened to whisk his mind's eye into an unremembered part of his life.

"Horatio," an older, punk haired woman inquired. The tips of pink accented the black.

"Yes?"

"Welcome to the Sanctuary," she said with an extended arm. After a quick shake she moved her arm out for Horatio to drink in the grandeur. Her jagged hair stood in stark contrast to the blue and green robes that were draped over her body.

The garden, it could be called, had to be about ten acres. Between fruit trees, vegetables, and bushes, were grassy knolls that people lazed in. Some held books in the air, others laid on their stomachs in quiet slumber. A small amount of people sat in front of their canvass'. It was clear the scenery was only a muse, and not the subject. All under the luminescent glow of countless lights.

"What is this."

"Just as it's called, sanctuary. We all maintain this whole facility in some way or another. And it's highly recommended to work here after the more gruelling research that goes on upstairs. Please help yourself darling, you look famished."

Horatio had been staring at the plot of tomatoes, their weight pulled the plants low. Vegetables, and fruits of all kinds crowded the narrow dirt path they walked. "Thank you," he said as he glanced between her and the food. Unsurety held his feet only a second before he fell to a knee, and picked one. The first bite stung his mouth, the acidic sugar blend overwhelmed at first, but as the juice began to drip off the corners of his mouth it had combined into an unmatched savory treat. So long had he subsisted on gruel that the taste made him want to cry. What his ancestors easily cultivated, was a cherished treasure for him. "People would kill for this."

Her somber tone broadsided Horatio, "people have died for this. This, our birthright." Irritation held her face for only a second as Horatio saw her recall their history in an instant. "But that is not why you are here," she said with a smile. "You're here to meet Horace."

"Yeah, uh, Fred mentioned him." Horatio continued to eat as they moved through the garden. As he swallowed down, a realization prompted a question. "So my team. Our base. One of many for you?"

61

She halted her step, "Your team has been the only one operating for the last fifteen years. Ever since," her words stopped at the appearance of a walking boulder. "Horace," she said questioningly to herself. "Horace," she proceeded to shout and wave to the man. Horatio barely saw him return a small wave. They proceeded toward him.

His breath could be described as a wheeze at best. His hand engulfed Horatio's as he gave him a hearty damp shake. He placed his other oversized wet hand on top of the shake. "Damn pleasure to meetcha. Gone through a lot of your team's work. But no use in hashin' up the past. Just yet at least." He looked over to the woman with a chortle, "Victoria! Helpin out our friend here?" She smiled graciously with a nod. "Well that clocks a'runnin. Gotta get some medicine in you. Look like you've been through," he had a small coughing fit as he bent to retrieve a handful of carrots, "hell." His sleeve slid across his mouth before he offered up a carrot to Horatio. He devoured it. With a forced smile, Horace offered up another. The pain of which Horatio noted with gratitude.

"Thank you so much," he said with a mouthful of carrot. They began to walk, Victoria had already begun collecting vegetables. Her robe was her basket.

"Don't let her grace fool you, she's a real bearcat."

"Bearcat?"

"Yeah it's when, uh, never mind. Come on inta the saloon."

Horatio had passed from the garden to a graveled parameter, an awning of wood crested the

62

top. He had just then noticed doors scattered along the outside. Different colored doorways stood out against the concrete walls of the immense "room" of the garden. The double doors in front of him were the only one of their kind though. Horace shimmied through sideways, his body rubbed as the doors creaked against their hinges.

The saloon was simplicity, though robustly stocked with ten large decanters shelved on the far wall. One corner held a circular table, while the rest of the space was taken up with various style chairs. "Have a sit huh," Horace grunted, moving to the shelves. "Name your poison."

"Saquila, if you have it," Horatio put his head down. He ruffled up his hair, then rubbed his fingers together. He wondered if they had cleaning water.

Horace laughed, "Yeah, yeah we got that. Most common round these parts. Go down south, down deep in there, you'll find Rin all day long. Squeezin limes into their Rin, all day long." Horace's movements stopped as he had been whisked completely and utterly away to his yesteryears.

"Limes?"

"Huh," Horace looked startled, a smile bloomed. "Right then, just takes me back. Ya'know? We weren't always fighters ya'know. You weren't always a fighter, where you?"

"I thought we weren't hashing up the past."

Horace handed him a drink in sloppy fashion, splashing droplets onto both. "Out in those beatin lights? No, can't reflect out there. Need to go deep into yourself. Need to loosen up to do that though." He gave an equally sloppy salute with his glass. A big glass of Rin. Did he have that lime in there?

Horatio was always curious about new foods or drinks.

"Thank you," Horatio said giving a small salute back, and tilted down the first half. He reeled, clenched his mouth, he almost doubled over from the cough fit. "Is this bad? I think you, I think there's something wrong with this."

"Drink the rest, there's nothin wrong with it." Horace said as he stared at his own drink with contemplative tones.

Horatio, still with the idea of wriggling off the mortal coil, gave no hesitation to the second half. The glass dropped. He wretched, thankful none of the small amount of food he had came up. "No, there's something definitely wrong with that."

"There really isn't, you're just tastin the ayahuasca, nothin really covers that up ya'know?"

Drugs weren't unheard of, but the mention of the hallucinogen to Horatio may as well had been to state he had put bird in the drink. You could go to any dead body on the street, and find cocaine. Marijuana and cigarettes much harder to come by. Pills? That supply was endless. Hallucinogens, however, had practically been eradicated. When the world created their fantasy they had no use to go inside their own head.

"I, I mean, I've only really ever smoked a little. Maybe a few bumps."

"Are you scared?"

Horatio didn't know what he was, was this a trick? Was Horace's melting glass a placebo induced vision? He laughed, slapped his knee, and covered his face with both hands. It was hilarious to him.

"You weren't always a fighter, were you?"

The words rippled their way to Horatio. He looked at Horace. The hairs of his robust beard twisted, and curled. The lines next to his brown eyes deepened. He was a caricature. The words reverberated again.

***

The door slid open instantly for Mira, and Frederick. Mira didn't feel the coolness, but did note there was a twenty degree drop in temperature. "Is this where we'll work on the overdrive?"

"Overdrive? No, I assure you, Olympe will cull out all the little secrets it's hiding. We're here to work on you." Frederick turned his back to her as he busied himself an oblong shaped table that jutted out of the wall. It held a variety of metallic instruments.

"Me," Mira questioned, her instinct was to run, but held herself still.

"We have a unique opportunity. That is, if you enjoyed your little rampage."

Mira loosened herself a little, "Enjoyed would be an understatement."

"Excellent!"

"No! No, it's not. It was a drug. I could have drowned myself in it."

"You cut the enemy."

"I killed innocents."

Frederick's palms were flat on the table, he had stopped working. "Innocents are dying now. In horrific ways. You're a testament to that." He turned away to equipment he didn't need, her red eyes had frightened him, a momentary flair before they resumed their emerald hue.

"You're right, I am. Even before they turned me into this monstrosity."

Frederick hard swallowed as he turned back around to face her, but looking downward at tools. Busying himself once more. "I was there too, your family saved my life." Mira moved away from him, instead studying the three mechanical arms that hung lifelessly above a surgical table. "I just want to end this," he continued.

She had already been burned at the stake, her ashes shoved in the mechanical suit she found herself in. If her hand could not touch, but could scorch. If she could not dance, but destroy. If she heard, and saw everything instead of the small chunks and fragments that led so many people into their delusions. Who was she to keep these humanities when her humanity had already been ripped from her. It was an illusion she chose to dissolve.

"I want to end this too."

***

Horatio drifted in darkness. He felt calm, was this death? His eyes opened at the sound of a pop, it was exquisitely sharp. Below him where basketball sized bubbles that drifted listlessly upwards. They were innumerable. Images glided over the translucent surface of the bubbles, distorted images of places and people in his life. He saw her, a face of determination cut from stone. It came close to him, but he contorted himself to avoid the thought.

66

Another, an image of her in tears barely missed him as he bent his back. He felt his spine crack. His breath caught, had he broken his back? He laid hunched in the void, a bubble lifted towards him. Tears came to his eyes as he watched it come for him. Her words inaudible as the scene of her speaking played out. She was upset, he knew the moment. It engulfed his head.

"My father's influence is getting us nowhere!"

Horatio's soul was a spectator, he stood in the pupil of his former self's eye, his sight locked on the love of his life. "Well Catherine," *God please don't! Stop! Stop you fucking fool!* "We could join the Mutinist."

"You would join?" Her smirk dug into his conscious. He burned alive in his own anguish.

"I'd sign in blood, someone's got to look out for you." His laugh echoed. Horatio felt it bounce in his head, covered his ears, fell to his knees, clenched his eyes. The pull came instantly, ripped forward in time. His body felt on the verge of being torn apart.

"Go! it's a trap!" Catherine's words rang out. Horatio stood in shocked horror. The mechanical hand had dropped the instant the room was illuminated. It shot out to grip her mid sprint, metal fingers that were curled open, in a second, tightened. Her feet and arms jerked forward as her midsection was grabbed and pulled back. The crack of broken bones came in three loud snaps. His ears went numb to her screams. Paralyzed, her arms hung limp. He stood under her, his body shook, petrified. Her wail finally broke the static, it came in an amplified tone. Another hand dropped, it's index finger resembled a scissor. It flipped out, and moved in a fluid motion. Catherine's head lifted up then down into its metal palm. The hand moved back to its origin, the trophy secure, before the first gush of blood shot up. The other let the body fall towards Horatio, baptizing him in her blood. Only a moment passed before her life began to sizzle his flesh. A million blood cells glued to his body. Immolated him, boiled him down into the ground.

His soul floated in a river of red. Words he had half heard from his teammates were now in clear focus. Dictation of his listlessness, half-finished sentences, and uneasy words. He swam away, he hadn't listened before, he wasn't about to start. Faster he moved, a salmon against the tide that pulled. The crimson viscous river gave no warning of its end, Horatio leaped out and over the edge.

A click, he turned. The door was closed. He remembered the moment instantly. Where he had chosen to die. To stay behind while the team retreated to safety, and Mira took the train. He turned, the multi-colored council faced him. Time skipped, he held the two wires in his hand. Ten seconds flashed on the screen. He stepped back. A thud pulled his attention toward the corner of the room. A bot stepped out of the shadow.

"Catherine?" he questioned out. She ran to him, embraced him. Electricity filled the air. Small arks peppered the room. The core was in the midst of going red hot. Time snailed by. The energy, a white wall, inched towards them. She held him close, a bubble formed.

They were surrounded by light, she looked into his wet eyes. Her gold colored hair covered her left eye, the other still held it's hazel hue. A shiver shot as she placed her hands on his arms. Pulled in close, he could only stare in disbelief. "Protect Mira," a whisper that rang in the silence of their haven. The bubble popped.

Horatio woke with a start, a soft blue hue filtered through the open windows of the saloon. Horace's glass was filled again. He tilted it towards Horatio, "Welcome back."

Horace's words fell on deaf ears as Horatio vomited over the side. He laid back, his breath short. He fought the tears only a moment before he began to sob.

***

Mira's eyes opened, the room was dimly lit, a few candles scattered about. "What time is it," she asked to Olympe without turning her head. The answer came instantly to her mind, but she still waited for Olympe's response. She was acutely aware of anyone within fifty feet. The activity of Verite buzzed her senses, and that was as low as her functions could operate. She liked it.

"Afternoon, around 1."

Mira sat up in her cot, she looked at her decision. Her left hand gone, replaced with an egg like cylinder. The white sheen held her eyes, it looked sleek she dared to think. She wasn't one for vanity, but destruction could be beautiful. Removing the sheet revealed her new mechanical legs. Their obsidian color contrasted perfectly with her hand. She had always had an affinity for the monochromatic.

"Removing the faux flesh, and blood allowed us to use slightly more metal to reinforce your legs with a titanium shielding. You're unstoppable in traditional terms."

"I'm unstoppable on every term," Mira said. Her statement shocked herself.

"Mira," she said with a tilted head, "the hubris of humankind has always been their downfall."

She went to clench her hands, her right obeyed, her left powered up. She quickly dispelled it. Olympe smiled. "Sorry," Mira muttered.

"Your mind is connected to such power you can control your own reality. That means you must be vigilant of your own thoughts, doubly so. You understand?"

Mira didn't speak, her head hung. She did understand, but that didn't make her want to listen. Mira, in that moment, understood exactly what she meant, but her stubbornness was equal to her will. She let go with a sigh. "I do. I've been running on unending scorn, hate, passion. Sometimes I fear it's the only fuel I know."

"I'm not saying douse your light, on the contrary light every field afire. Do it with passion, but use logic. Hate of the ideals, not those who have been fooled to hold them. Remember being scorned, but do not scorn. I promise, holding that balance will create more than enough fire for you to use. And I believe in your use."

Mira finally raised her eyes to look at Olympe, "Thank you. We will end this."

"That will only be the byproduct of the beginning you start. Focus more on that, it's more important than the ending." Mira nodded. They raised, and hugged. "Now let's meet with Frederick, and Horatio." Mira was the machine, but Olympe was the one that seemed to float, perfect movement. She couldn't take her eyes off of her, Mira questioned herself to figure the obsession, and found it in the root of truth. There were no airs, and everything was just as Olympe was able to relate to her. Verite was the fifth or sixth seed, but she always poured all her resources into them. What her and her team fought years for, what they died for. Mira knew in her soul they were all ghosts, Horatio and herself included. Verite, and Olympe could be half of their current stature, and Mira would have found it Nirvana still.

As Mira's life had stated, all she knew was the vilification of humans. She either dealt with it, ran from it, or hunted it on a daily basis. The last of humans with humanity she knew were dead. In fact the grief of which had made her completely forget of Olympe, and the dream she had no idea was still standing or not. Not that she would have ever admitted to her team she had, on occasion, held reservations on the validity of Verite. That Olympe could have died, and been replaced with Luminescent. They separated so long ago, and communication was mostly one sided as she funneled tech, and information to them. Now that the paranoia had been cleared up her faith double downed.

Upon their entrance, the first thing Mira noted was Horatio's laissez faire attitude. His relaxed demeanor made him older for some reason. She hadn't seen him laugh in ages. There he sat in a small group with Frederick, and Horace. The two stifled their laughing as Horace continued. Mira, and Olympe joined in, Mira held her hands behind her back. Thankful the jeans hid her legs.

"So she's gotten the Lumen's Hand all riled up, and her Pa says, 'shut yer yap, I just a mind to send you with them.' She looks right at him, and says 'Or put a wig on you, and have a real dandy of a time.' The group laughed.

"What happened then?" Horatio asked.

"Oh, uh, she poisoned all their drinks and killed them."

"Well," Olympe intervened, "I think Frederick has some great news."

"Sure do," he said with a rise. His lips curled up uncontrollably as he talked, "the overdrive gave us a treasure trove of memories, from one of the insiders, to the whole system. The device did seem to have a 5 year deletion cycle system, which makes us question the humanity of these leaders. I mean to only hold memories for up to 5 years, how could you make connections to anyone, or any ideas. But we are not here for philosophical questions, the real bread and butter is that we have found."

Frederick removed a small device from his lab coat, he held it up to allow a holographic map pop up. "Exact coordinates to the main Processing Center. We can, once, and for all reveal what happens to the people being sent there. With that footage, there isn't a person on this planet that wouldn't revolt." His exuberance held as he looked around the room for reactions.

"Weapons?" Mira asked. Frederick tilted his head slightly as he locked eyes. Mira looked to Horatio.

"Right, right. We do have something in store for Horatio. The rest of the team however won't be armed."

"What," Horatio's eyebrows peaked.

"We weren't even going to have any weapons for the original mission. It should be a simple in, and out. We're just adding in the destruction since it's an option. Hopefully it'll have some disruptive effect."

Silence held the room only a moment before Mira nodded, "It makes sense." Horatio followed suit in agreement. They continued their discussion of the imminent attack. The infiltration group had been created even before they had went to secure the overdrive. Now with Mira and Horatio, Olympe and Frederick felt relieved. As they stepped aside with Horace to discuss Verite matters, Horatio immediately hugged Mira. "This place is worth every sacrifice we've ever made." Mira put her arms tightly around her friend. As they pulled apart Horatio finally noticed her completely.

"What happened," He asked, another step back.

"Oh this? These? Just some modifications."

"You chose this?"

"Yes Horatio, I chose this." A small sigh escaped her. "This is bigger than us."

Horatio glanced down to his pocket, "You're right. Well captain, ready to do this?" He smiled at her, a genuine smile. Her head tilted to process it, had his smile come to be that foreign to her?

Chapter 6
Catechism

Gustav rolled his head back, stretched out his neck, and rubbed his eyes.

"You ok Cap?"

"Yeah, neck's... yeah I'm fine." He looked at his team. Their eyes drooped, fingers twitched, all ready to about face to bed. "Frie, guard the parameter," Gustav grunted.

"Captain?"

"You heard me soldier."

"Hey Cap, let's not make this a knife to gun fight, yeah?" Misant immediately regretted her words.

"Right, it won't have a chance against Frie!" Carthy gave a smile, putting a hand on Frie's real shoulder. When her eyes met with Gustav's she dropped them, and her hand of support.

"So, the Mutinist truly does breed dissent. She has you all so frightened as to not follow orders?" He paced over his troops. Eyed them for what was next.

Pierce finally opened his mouth, "Gustav, please don't be bullheaded. This bot isn't normal." His words were reluctant. He stepped up to Gustav.

He chuckled to himself, his oldest... Gustav's thought had to pause to categorize him. Confidant? Now his confidant questioned him. He laughed a bit, cracked his knuckles, and twisted his neck with a loud pop. The worn leader turned his back to them, could he just leave them all out here? No, a mission with so many variables couldn't be completed by one person.

He turned, fire touching his face. His brain was heated from the stims, and the euphoric high that kept him awake quickly morphed to unbridled rage. "It's one bitch!" he shouted out incredulously as he turned. Incognizant faces stared back at him.

Pierce looked at him puzzled, "No," he said taken aback, "It's a bot. They don't have genders. They aren't human."

Gustav nodded slowly, locking eyes with him. He questioned his use of stims with a slip like that. "You just have no idea," he paused, "how weak they are." He stepped out from his team, arms spread open. "But you are making them so strong right now. Your fear is incapacitating you. Questioning your leader, dissent in the ranks" he spat the last part. He took a breath, then barked out, "Misant."

"Sir," she piped out.

"You ever kill a bot?"

"No, Sir."

"Humans?"

Her eyes dropped, "Sir! Yes, Sir!" She forced out her reluctant reply with exuberance.

"Well it's a lot easier to kill a bot. One electrical hit and they are down. Can you say that about a human? Tasers, and bullets cannot break the will of a man with obsession, we've all seen that. How many of us had to blow the brains out of some junkie as the only way to stop them?"

He moved around his team. "Frie, have you killed a junkie in that fashion?"

"Sir. Yes, Sir."

"Carthy, have you had to kill a junkie in that fashion?"

"Sir. Yes, Sir."

He paused in step, in front of Misant, "Have you killed a junkie in that fashion?"

"Sir." her voice quivered.

"Sir, what," he said with ice in her face.

"Sir. Yes, Sir."

He turned to Pierce, "Report, now, how many have you killed in this fashion."

"Four hundred twelve separate incidents," Pierce said as he stared straight ahead. Into the brilliant lights of the city they fought for. He had always thought they were on the same team, humanity's team, but the forced retrospection put a seed of doubt in him.

"More kills than days in a year. And that's just the junkies. That's not even tallying up the insurgents. We obliterated the Mutinist, and her team for Christ's sake!"

He walked through his rank one last time, "Pierce, Misant, Carthy enter that building, now." They moved in quick succession into the building.

"Frie, guard the parameter." Heat continued to hold Gustav's brain. He knew it was just a woman, her brain scrambled up, and served. But would they accept it. Would he risk Frie going rogue? *Didn't Luminescent think of anything*! He suddenly feared he was talking out loud, but was reassured he had only screamed in his head. Forty had crept up on him years ago, the all nighters had begun to take their toll.

The sun had just started to rise, but the thicket of skyscrapers held the darkness. Gustav came up the rear. He held eyes with Frie a few moments before he entered. Could he bull-dog a bot? Gustav's com went off as they entered the building, "They've breached the processing center. They're destroying it. Your team now has red access. Neutralize them at all cost." Just as he thought.

"Understood. Team, move out." They filed into the elevator of a lobby that was as nondescript as the next. Gustav knew what laid below them, however his team had no idea. Nor had they even stopped to consider the possibility. He was equal parts curious, and fearful of their reactions. The elevator lurched downward.

***

"Ready to breach Captain."

The statement made her feel uneasy, there was a dissonance between her team now, and the one that had all but been obliterated. The faces of the dead floated over the new members. Where her memories being projected, could they see that? Was that the cause of all of Horatio's uneasy looks? She knew that they weren't attackers, and that's what ate at her. If only it wasn't just her, and Horatio with a weapon. Though she had to concede that if the mission went according to plan, the only one causing destruction would be herself. Contained, and just of the structure. No casualties this time.

Mira nodded. The thermite lit in a spectacular brilliance. The light of which made everyone but her close their eyes. She cleared the distance in an instant, her feet flung out against the metal. It blasted out, a perfect circle of where the thermite had perforated. She rode the chunk of metal as it slid into the room. *Finally*. Raising up her eyes scanned the facility, she stood in horror.

The ceiling was filled with women. They dangled from the domed ceiling in mechanized hands. Motorized fingers that clutched them like dolls. Underneath floated nine immense globules. Vibrant chartreuse spheres that hung in space between the mechanical sky, and a sea of conveyor belts and bots. The blobs held some gelatinous liquid. Their work was horrific, Mira watched the process as an occupied hand fell into the liquid. Dipped in, only a few seconds would pass before they awoke in terror. Eyes bulging as their body convulsed. The claw held them still as they tried to squirm out. Black tears bled from their eye-ducts. Soon after it flowed from her ears, and mouth as well. A tar like substance that collected in the middle. Then, from its weight, fell out of globule. Its final destination the mouth of the bot held under it. The conveyor belt moved, dumped the bot, and repositioned a new one.

"What are they doing to them?" Coraline asked in a daze. She watched the spiralled conveyor belts, each one positioned under a globule. Most of the bots on the conveyor belts were the flagship model, but there were males and females of varying ethnicities scattered throughout. The three from Verite stepped forward only a few feet, terror and helplessness held them. Benjamin, and Dantes grabbed Coraline as she began to mindlessly venture further. They looked to Mira, who still stood staring, silenced by her thoughts.

"Captain," Benjamin questioned.

78

"Begin recording, Horatio and I will try to get a sample of this substance." Mira responded without removing her gaze. She could hear the two try and snap Coraline out of shock. The whole point of their organization was on the foundation that something like this was happening, but the brutality of it astonished all of them. As a hand withdrew with the husked body, it simply went into the dome for disposal, and returned with a new live sleeping subject. The newly arrived unconscious waited for their turn. The processing center seemed to operate non-stop, ten bots had already been created since they had breached the door. After they were out of hearing distance Mira questioned Horatio, "Can you believe this? Hey. Horatio?"

His attention had slipped a million miles. Had this been done to Catherine? Instead of a body, her head dumped in the green goop before him. Her essence ripped from her. Mira's hand on his shoulder brought him back. "No, I can't believe this. There's something wrong here."

"What do you mean?" Mira continued to work. She didn't have to reach far, the walkway they were on passed right by a globule. She touched the tube to it, astonished as it was sucked in. It lingered for a bit in the substance, then fell down and out. Did she dare get it on her hand?

"I mean this isn't adding up. I'm alive, you're alive. Look at this, there's no reason we are alive, but for they want us to be. You certainly weren't created like this. Why?"

She stared at the green mass, "They? The Luminescent?" The footsteps cut their conversation.

"We have footage of everything. Pictures, and," Benjamin looked at his peer in annoyance.

"Captain," Coraline interrupted.

"Coraline."

"I know the orders are to destroy this place, but..." she lingered, "we'll kill all these people!"

Mira looked down, she hadn't even considered that she'd be killing all the women hanging on the ceiling. Embarrassment stung her cheeks. She really must know if she blushes or not. Mira had become giddy at the idea of destroying this facility. To bring down this slight against humanity. Destruction flowed in her veins now, she wanted more. She couldn't give in.

Now Dantes interrupted, "They're going to a fate worse than death, all we're doing is releasing them from that."

"It's not right!"

"It's the only right thing to do!"

"Silence." Mira had crossed her arms, she had no idea what to do. Her head down, she tried to repel the extra sensory perceptions and focus on her humanity. The ceiling overloaded her. The loss of life killed her. She looked to Horatio, he was back in his own world. "We need to neutralize these globules. Do not, I repeat, do not get any of it on you. They must be held in place with magnetics, we need to disable," her words were cut short by a bolt of electricity that smacked her in the chest. She flew into Horatio.

"Mira, Mira!" Horatio shook her with his free arm, his other arm pinned under her mechanical body.

80

Gustav lowered his electric rifle, the team held their HPB rifle's pointed at the insurgents.

"Mutinist, we must stop meeting like this." Gustav smirked as Mira's eyes were static with an array of colors, her body tremored. Horatio struggled to free his arm, and his weapon. "You're all under arrest, lower your weapons."

"You mean our cameras? We aren't here to fight, we're here to expose the truth." Coraline now positioned herself between Mira and Gustav. "Look around, how can you justify this?"

"I'm not here to justify the Luminescent's plan, just enforce it."

"This is bullshit, you can't agree with that," she pleaded, her chest touched against Misant's barrel.

Misant, and Carthy looked at each other. His face was torn, she widened and narrowed her eyes. She pleaded in her heart and head, but knew what he was about to do.

"Don't!" Misant was already mid-twist as Carthy cried out her warning. Gustav was quick. He gripped the nozzle of the gun, jammed the butt of the rifle into Misant's face, and ripped it away. Misant was doubled over, clutching at his face that dripped with blood. Gustav brought the butt down hard against his teammate's head. Misant was out cold. He looked over at Carthy who trembled as she held her rifle pointed at him.

"Put it down Carthy."

"No," her voice shook, "this is wrong! What the hell is going on here. Are all those bots really people?"

Gustav stared, he contemplated murdering everyone, but Pierce. Luminescent would probably give him a raise. He jumped, his hand struck her throat in a blur. A crack rang out. She fell, her hands scratched at her throat as she tried to gasp for air. He picked her up, an act of mercy in his mind, and threw her into the organic orb.

Her face contorted, and limbs flailed wildly. She tried to scream. Two seconds ticked by. Everyone stared as the black oil hemorrhaged out of her eyes, mouth, and ears. The substance went to its new home, and Carthy's lifeless body dropped out of the goo. It hit hard against the conveyor belt, and rolled off.

Pierce drew his baton, the electrical hum warned Gustav. He sidestepped, brought his fist down against Pierce's wrist. The baton flew out of his hand, and off the side as the two began fighting. In the years spent with each other, it was nothing for Gustav's jab to be pushed aside, and Pierces elbow to be ducked. They went back and forth, seemingly choreographed at lightning speed. Gustav ended it when he brought his foot down against Pierce's knee, the breaking of bones rang out. Red took over his sight as he saddled his friend. The thought of the word boiled his blood as he twisted him around and began to slam his fists down. Blood came quickly. He lifted him up, "Does loyalty mean nothing to you!" He spit into his comrades face before moving to throw him into the same glob he threw Carthy.

Pierce fell as a beam disintegrated Gustav's elbows. He held what was left of his arms up with shocked short breath, his burnt flesh lingered in the air. Mira stood with a hand on the rail, her egg pointed at him. Gustav turned to run. Another thinner beam shot through his right foot, entering the heel, and obliterating toes. He fell to his chest, a cry of anguish finally escaped. He attempted to crawl.

Mira pointed her hand-cannon at him, she was going to murder him. Energy built quickly, and illuminated her angered face. "Die!"

Pierce threw himself into Mira's arm, the beam cut into the walkway. It shuddered but held. He fell back, the beam's heat burnt his shoulder. Cloth melted into his shoulder. He winced as he attempted to stand, his good arm stretched out to calm. "Please," he breathed heavy, "please! You have your evidence just leave. Leave, and fix this."

Mira looked to her team, Horatio held by her side as they shielded the group from Verite. He had extended his wrist mounted shell spurter. It'd blast a hole through any chest, man or machine. "Fine. Go, take your leader," she couldn't hide the contempt behind the last word. Pierce nodded, he moved back. Taciturnity filled the air.

"What happened," the question cut the silence. Frie stood at the blasted entrance, feet from Gustav who reached out with his burnt elbow.

"Kill them all," Gustav sputtered out. He reached in agony with his other elbow only to pass out.

Frie threw out his arm, an energy blast careened chaotically from his palm. It flashed towards the group of insurgents. They all ducked down except Coraline. She dropped to her knees, her jawbone exposed. Half her face had been obliterated, her brain and nasal cavity were charred cross section. Dantes scrambled to her, picked her up into his arms. Benjamin sat dazed his eyes locked on the risen smoke. Mira didn't need to look to see a lost life signature, she gave a stop order to Horatio as she charged her left arm. His hand trembled in anger as he held the grip of his gun.

"Wait! Please everyone wait," Pierce yelled out, "Frie, don't listen to Gustav. Look at what they are doing."

Frie, like the rest of the team, had not been behind the curtain. The process, which hadn't stopped, continued churning out bots from live people. Frie drank in the hellish landscape. "What is this," he asked.

"You see what it is," Pierce spat. "We've been lied to."

Mira let go of her energy. She stood slowly.

"Captain, Coraline's dead! Do something!" Dantes had stood now, his hands were fists.

Frie turned, "Pierce, you did this to Gustav?" His brain hurt. He could hear another voice. He touched his head.

"Look at what's going on, we can't defend this." Pierce limped cautiously to his newly mechanized partner. He stepped pass Gustav carefully, still fearful regardless of his state. "You ok?" The question barely escaped his mouth when Frie's eyes rolled to the back of head. Contorting ferociously, his mechanical arm jutted in a curvature. Five fingers punctured Pierce's chest. A bolt of energy from the palm ripped through him, and sent him over the rail of the walkway. Controlled, Fried continued his onslaught.

Mira threw her cylinder up, but Frie threw out his hand in another curvature, the jet of energy crossed before Mira's feet. Instantly the walkway twisted and groaned in front of Mira. He put both arms into the air. His seemingly normal hand opened in the middle. Two more jets cut through globules, claws, and women. Limbs, goo, and metal rained down. He gripped Gustav, walking back out of the entrance. The walkway continued to slowly dip down towards the floor which had started to get covered by the mysterious liquid. Mira's feet tore through her shoes, and gripped into the honeycombed metal of the walkway, she clutched onto the grate as Horatio. Benjamin, Dantes all used her for support. They were almost vertical as Coraline's body finally rolled onto them. The added weight caused her feet rip through her metal perch. They all dropped to the floor. Everyone groaned out as they stood except Mira. The lights went out, red flashes illuminated the area. Sirens blared.

"Run," Mira shouted. They were in the middle of the room, and the globules had lost whatever power that sustained their suspension. The three scrambled over the spiralled conveyor belts, Mira made two calculated leaps to reach the nearest wall. She cocked her hand up, and blasted a hole. She looked back. Dantes held Coraline's body against his back, her arm slung over his shoulder. Large blobs of the green goo had already started to rain down. One splashed in front of him. He halted. Mira felt her feet planted in frustration. Benjamin, and Horatio turned as they cleared the last conveyor belt. A splotch of green goo fell on top of Dante's, and Coraline, the weight of which brought him down. His convulsions began immediately. Horatio dragged Benjamin by the arm towards the blasted escape.

Almost all of the foul liquid had fallen by the time they reached their exit, they hurried down the corridor as it crept after them.

"Ben, where do we go," Mira asked. Horatio, and Ben were out of breath.

"Uh, fuck, I don't know, which way is forward?"

"East, that way is east," she said with her finger extended outward.

Ben spun, tried to remember the schematics he thought he had memorized. "North, we need to go North, he sputtered and pointed to the wall left of them. Mira felt the consolidation of energy. She fell back with Horatio as a blinding light blasted through the ceiling. Nothing was left of Benjamin.

Frie dropped through the hole, onto the scorch mark that was their comrade. Mira had already gathered energy. She fired a fat pulse Frie barely moved around, his shoulder badly scorched. He threw one back, catching her in the chest. She flew back, her shirt burnt away leaving blackened metal. She grunted lifting her arm. Another blast flew out that Frie avoided, but hit Mira's mark. A newly created exit that beckoned them.

Horatio lost no time, and pulled a syringe from his shirt pocket, jamming it into himself. He felt his blood on fire, moving quickly before the beast could send another blast. He punched out, the circular wrist cannon shot 6 12-gauge shredder shells into Frie's midsection, blood and oil showered around them. He stumbled back, and kicked a leg out. Horatio moved aside, and brought his cannon against the outstretched limb. It flew off, and spattered Horatio's face in blood and bits of bone. He fell back, and down with a thud.

Horatio jumped, reeled his arm back, and brought it down hard against his head. Obliterated, blood misted and the cavity oozed. Horatio breathed heavy still on top of the fallen agent. He turned, looked to Mira. He let out a little laugh. "Shit, Mira. You ok?

Relief was short lived as Frie jerked alive, raising itself up. Horatio felt an arm swing around his back, Mira's shouts were drowned out by instant fear. Metal fingers clamped around his wrist. In a moment his arm was ripped away, and flung to the floor. The headless body pushed Horatio away, and threw out its hand out. The ball of energy caught Mira off guard, twisting her shoulder into it. The force of it blasted her hard against the wall, blurred her vision. Clothes and faux flesh gave way, exposing more of her metallic body.

Thoughts stabbed her repeatedly. Mira couldn't power up her arm. She fell back, crawled away from him. Frie was a monstrosity, his leg and neck oozed a mixture of blood and oil as he crawled his way to Mira. A relentless puppet, void of any consciousness. Focusing did nothing, she had learned the truth only to die with it.

Horatio shook on the floor, he fumbled to his pocket. His breath was short, he forced air to enter and exit his lungs. He jammed the remaining two vials into himself. The effect was instant, feeling shot out of his body, time slowed. He went for his cannon. His foot held the weapon down as he wrenched his arm out. In an instant it was on his right hand, his steps feral as he ran.

The mechanoid closed in on Mira. Horatio leapt, landing hard on its back. His fist slammed down into it. He punched again, and again. Blood and oil threatened to drown him as it drenched his face. He was covered, unable to open his eyes as he rolled off onto his back. Mira stared at Horatio, her back against the wall. Convulsions quickly overtook his body as foam came to his mouth.

Mira ran to him, her hand touched his shoulder, a diagnostic of his blood flared up.

"What is this, what did you take? Horatio? Damnit answer me!" She almost brought her hand down on his chest, but the thought of her strength made her stop. "I'm sorry," she whispered. She charged her arm, using a concentrated beam to cauterize his wound. The blood stopped. Mira lifted him over her shoulder, and carried him out their exit.

Chapter 7
Sanctuary

Horatio floated in a dark abyss. Nothingness invaded his body, which prompted a serious thought that he may in fact be dead. Another realization came; he very well could have died in the explosion days ago. Forced to chase one in a million chances in a purgatory just above hell. A cage he'll never be free of. He had to figure out why he was doomed. Why he was repeatedly forced to come so close to have it all ripped away. Perhaps this was it. He Perseus, this fight his boulder.

The thought terrified him, he curled into himself even more until he caught a glimpse. A light, angelic even. Her face, she was finally there, there to comfort him. Every idea he had ever fought for, she had fought for first. Breathed revolution into his soul. She desired to create a new reality, and that spoke to him. Because of that he was eternally grateful.

Horatio ran to her with no thought, or floated would be more apt. Her face, a sweet loving portrait, faded fast. Catherine morphed, a demon's mouth opened to swallow him whole. He fell down the beast's gullet.

Stomach acid poured over his skin, it burned him, his flesh. Skin dripped off to reveal his muscle tissue. Which also quickly disintegrated. Bones. Nothing. All that remained were his thoughts, he was in darkness once more. Her face was there again, he ran through the void. Mira was there, fighting, surely could he save Catherine's soul by joining.

Suddenly he was with her, they were unstoppable. Waving swords of light, they cut through shadows. Shadows of themselves. Shadows of their friends. Each slash brought a cloud of dust, but dark souls surrounded them completely. The kills were easy, but it was an endless fight. Mira fell to a knee, they leapt and devoured her. He reached out, and in an instant was devoured too.

Another restart, darkness again. He floated in the abyss in strange deja vu. He saw Catherine, swam away only to encounter Mira. Desperation forced him up. Or somewhere that felt up to him. He wasn't swimming anymore, he dangled. His eyes could see the strings that held him. He floated down, his feet touching a primitive dilapidated theater. He hung there, hung with Catherine, and Mira. They moved to the tune of maniacal cackling. Catherine's strings were cut, and she fell dead. Mira's were cut, she fell dead. Horatio cringed as he fell to the ground, unable to breath, his eyes looked into Mira's. They lit green, she rose. He fell again, but this time with hope.

***

"And he's back," Olympe said as she moved from his bedside. She gave room for Mira to move in.

"Told ya Mira, he's a toughen."

"Come Horace, let's give them some space. Please come see me when you're done Mira."

Olympe put a hand on Horatio's shin, "I'm glad you're alright."

"Aye me too boy, get some rest." Horace exited sideways, Olympe drifted behind him. They closed the door.

"What were you thinking?" Her words frosted the room.

"I was thinking..." He raised a brow at her interruption.

"I had it under control," she interjected.

"Well I'm a creature of instinct, I'm sorry."

"You can't just rush in."

Horatio stared at Mira, heat started to rise in his voice, "You don't think I know all about rushing in? Don't you think I know the fucking costs!" He had lost it on the last sentence, his outburst irritated him more than Mira's lecture.

"You're right," her hostile gaze fell, "I apologize."

"I..."

"It's just that I don't want to lose any more family," she blurted out.

Horatio had worked with her since almost the beginning of her outfit, maybe thirteen years now. He had not heard her sound scared a day in that time. She was more human now then he had ever seen her. "I understand. The Luminescent keep ripping away our family to protect their secrets. But we can't give up, we can't let fear hold our feet. I made that choice because I believe in you. We are being manipulated, but I think you can rise outside of their schemes. I think you're the only one that can."

The last sentence slapped her. Mira stood, and walked towards the door. "Don't see Horace again, that's an order." She slammed the door behind her. *How could he put that pressure on me? He expects me to throw lives away so I'm the one to defeat them. To think fate links me, and no one else to this fight. I refuse to believe that!* Her fist dented the metal wall she struck out at. She held a moment before continuing on her way to Olympe's laboratory. As she turned a corner a body came fast. He fell back at striking her solid metal form. Mira looked down at him, the tears were still fresh on his face.

It was at that moment that Mira had regretted her choice to become the monster. Her eyes saw every detail of him. The click of the slow moving door indicated he had just left Olympe's office. A loved one of the departed. Hate vibrated in subtle fluctuations. His jaw clenched ever so slightly. A quick quiet apology that cried malevolence in volumes unheard. He moved passed her, head down, hurried steps echoed behind her. She didn't move, the picture of his blotched tear-stained face stuck in her mind's eye. Which translated to her literal eyes. The picture held over her pupils a moment longer before she forcefully dispelled it, and hurried to Olympe's door.

It was too easy for the pain to be transferred from him to her. Horatio's words replayed in hurried snippets. Mira closed her eyes, she felt on the verge of madness. A breath, relaxation flooded her with a new thought. She could walk away whenever she pleased. The idea raised her head, reinforced her sanity. Her hand held at the handle, she could turn around and leave. Never look back. Let Olympe and Frederick continue the fight, they were just as capable as her. She turned down the handle, her mind set to see Olympe, then leave.

* * *

Gustav's body lay on a metal medical table. His foot had been obliterated. His arms gone at the elbows. A dark suited woman walked towards him, she touched over what was left of him. A finger down his chest. She smiled. Her hair was aqua colored ice in a bun. Her black suit coat, and pants were perfectly tailored to her. The wings of her white blouse hung out. She jumped on him, a syringe filled with blue gel in her hand.

He woke with a start, the adrenaline and nanotechnology rebooted his heart and mind. His eyes saw a woman, light pierced his vision from above her. He forced one open, then the other. Valkyrie of Scelus, the savior of their world saddled him. She threw the syringe aside. "Matilda," he choked out.

"Gustav, we can save you, like we saved Frie. He died protecting you. Pierce as well, clearly an attempt to atone for his disobedience. Both slaughtered by the Mutinist. Tell me, Gustav, do you want your revenge?"

The pain didn't motivate him, he felt nothing with the drugs used on him. Instead, his mind felt free of his mortal bonds for a brief second. *Is my humanity my religion? And like all rigid system of beliefs holding me back?* It was a question he answered immediately. "Transform me, make me a god." Matilda hopped off, touched her fingers to his shoulder. He was flipped like nothing, his face against the cold metal table.

Agony pierced his whole body as she jammed the overdrive into his brain. Broke off the handle, and tossed the spent stick. Lights blinked above him, the mechanical arms descended from the ceiling as she left the room.

Gustav rested his face against the table, stared at the door Matilda had just walked through. The tools attached to the arms whirred to life, small laser beams started to cut into his flesh. He controlled his breath, for a moment. Another two hands came down, they each positioned behind a leg. Their beams began to cut just under his buttocks. His breath became rapid, he started to flail. Two restraints dropped down forcefully. Pinned him at his shoulders and back. He had to force breath into his lungs. On the verge of being crushed, he cried out. The dissection continued.

***

"Mira," Olympe said without turning around, "Thank you for coming so quickly, come look at this."

Mira stepped up behind her, she was staring at a video screen on her council. The video was an endorsement. With Gustav.

"There is a threat," he spoke over scenes of Mira's destruction, and the bots whose inhibitors she broke. "These mindless machines are imitating consciousness. They must be stopped. That's why

94

I've made the ultimate sacrifice, to become more than human. To become a Demi-god!"

"What is this? There's a ban on modification."

"Special decree, straight from the Council of Luminescent. People have been dying for this to be lifted."

Mira watched the video. *Where do I go, when I'll be hunted like a dog?* She felt the tentacles of fate wrap around her, they wanted to drown her. "I'm leaving." Her words raised Olympe's head.

"Very well, good luck Mira." She lowered her head, rewatched the video.

Mira stepped back. "Thank you," She turned. Her feet cemented. She forced movement, held her composure until she was out of sound. Then, began to run. She leapt as the railing came into sight, her newly patched coat flapped in the air. Pieces, and edges of it still remained burnt. Contact came hard, it echoed. Everyone in the cafe, and the denizens that walked around all stopped to stare. They watched her as she raised herself and moved towards the exit. They busied on.

The blast door that separated Verite from the abandoned subway tunnels was immense. The double reinforced doors had been cobbled together by the citizens of Verite. It looked worn, but was a solid barrier that would buy them enough time to evacuate should anything happen. A young kid, fourteen her intuition told her, sat at the small book sized control panel. The boy periodically looked at the screen by the door that displayed the other side of the entrance. He took notice of the new local attraction that walked towards him. "M...m Mira! It's you!"

Her smile felt forced, and quickly faded as she asked him to open the doors.

"Sure! When you come back, a bunch of us would love to hear some of your stories."

"Yeah," she lied. Her ears malevolently intensified the sound of the closing gate.

***

Horatio moved his new mechanical arm back, and forth. He brought his fist to his face, and opened his hand. He stared at his palm. Immediately he moved it away, the sensation of looking down a barrel of a gun swirled his thoughts. He laughed a little to himself.

"I'm glad your sense of humour is intact." Olympe was against the side of the opened door. "Horace is great with depression." Her mechanical eye swirled a multitude of hues purples, greens, and blues.

He laughed again, "I don't have depression."

Olympe smiled, "And you don't have post-traumatic stress disorder. Or anxiety."

His smile faded.

She held hers, for some reason it didn't patronize him. "It's ok. Did you ever think that was the point of society. Directed, and dictated? Going through horrible things is hard. Humans have categorized some of the symptoms, but we refuse to look at the root."

She stepped in, sat on the edge of the bed. She touched a finger to his temple. "Right there, the seat of consciousness. There's something in there, in us, that makes us aware. That awareness is not always of good things. Wouldn't it make sense processing so much bad, negative, evil will have an effect? We're humans, and if I recall correctly, even the Gods of the Greeks didn't have complete mastery of it." She laughed a little, covering her mouth as she always did, then turned back to him. "Do you know the origins of the call? The origins of Je ne se qua?"

Horatio shook his head, "I just know it was the call sign from the start."

"It was. Long before that though it meant someone who has it," she emphasised the last word. "Typically models. It was an x factor that made people adore them. Naturally it fell out of fashion though, as all things based on popularity, and became merely a relic of the past."

Olympe's real eye twisted up in thought, soft purple hues dominated the mechanical one now. "I suppose no one has anything special if everyone's embraced a singular idea. A thought that funnels everything through it." She broke off her train of thought, turned her attention back to Horatio, "Those that lived tortured lives not being able to create diversity sought it elsewhere. Namely, in their heads. Je ne se qua was resurrected as a term for acid between the few remaining names in the fashion industry. A market that had dwindled in a standardized world. They started the resistance against the Council of the Luminescent, almost a hundred years ago. Almost since the inception of the Council."

"The Council is everywhere, a force of so called light."

Olympe laughed, "If there's any light, it's only from the flames of their hate."

Horatio stared off, he contemplated her story. "Where's Mira?"

"Gone."

His head turned, "On a mission?"

"No."

"Dead? She died?!"

Olympe laughed, her hand again over her mouth. "Dear Horatio, she's gone. She left Verite. Nothing more, nothing less."

"You didn't stop her?"

"Why would I do that?"

"Why wouldn't you? We need her!"

Her sigh was heavy, "You know, in our line of work, you can't use the word need. Mira needed her parents, you needed Catherine, and we needed that footage. But we are perseverance, we fly in the face of adversity. You say we need her, I agree, however who am I to say that to her? The road to truth usually leads to one's demise. We're both aware of that. How can I force her to walk such a path?"

"I, but," he looked down, "she's my leader. I thought soldiers needed their leaders."

"And if she died? Would you not direct yourself?"

"Honestly? I don't know. I mean, I'd probably lay down and die too. You aren't tired? Tired of starting from nothing? Over and over?"

"Horatio, this is the fifth Verite. Mira, and her parents lived at one of them. She learned much, and admired the fight. Though we had never met, when her parents died she fulfilled their part of the protocol that had been established. She was the only one who did it, and thrived. The rest of the teams had been wiped out within weeks. I'd say her

98

passion surpassed her parents, but in their credit she was young and they were so very tired." Olympe's eyes drifted off. Lost in memory for a brief second, before her gaze turned back. "I am tired, but this is a fight against pure evil. A hate against humanity is being committed right now. I can only assure one fighter against it, myself."

Horatio nodded, "So that's when you started this one, when she went to establish her cell?"

"No I had two completely obliterated before here. But enough about this. I highly suggest you go down to the garden, and eat something." Olympe hugged him, "Hang in there." She raised and walked out. Her head poked back past the door frame, "Also we've taken the left sleeve out of your shirt, otherwise your power source in your shoulder would just make it catch fire. It's also flame retardant to help cut down that chance. You'll be fine. You should be fine."

Horatio stared at the space she left empty for a moment, was she being serious? He got out of bed, and looked at his shoulder. A bright spot could be seen if he moved his newly mechanized arm just right. He dressed, twisted and played with his arm a little more, then he made his way down to the garden.

Again the heavenly petrichor swept up his senses as he opened the door. To his immediate left were snap peas, he dropped down to eat them. After a handful he made his way further in, his eyes scanned for carrots as he walked through garden, and knolls. Again people were scattered about, in particular a large shape that slept underneath an apple tree had caught his eye. As Horatio approached Horace, he could see a half-eaten apple clutched in his palm. It looked the size of a plum in comparison.

"Getting in that beauty sleep?"

Horace dropped his apple as he woke with a startle. "Oh ho ya got me, figured you'd come round. Bout time for a drink huh?"

***

Mira didn't know where she was going, she walked blindly and loved it. She was in perfect condition, her surgery far faster than Horatio's with no healing time. The ability to kill anything or anyone in her path also had an easing effect. All she had to do was make it out of the city. She was already a good mile out. *Maybe I'll see birds, or dogs.* The thought made her giggle. A triggered memory of her parents reading to her. She hadn't had such a fantasy since her time with them.

Their demise created a call to circumstance that trumped her selfish curiosity then. She couldn't even say happiness, it really was for the sake of curiosity. A trait she cherished as her birthright. It would have been terrifying at the time, but she had always wanted to see outside of Scelus. Now she was perfectly equipped, nothing could stop her.

Mira's hand touched over the dilapidated seats of the traincar, a stuffed animal sat in one. Laid there, covered in dust. Her mind drifted towards the people back at Verite, over the people who she had recently seen eviscerated. Her mind, the perfect tool, gave her what she thought. All the death she had seen, crystal clear. A jolt of guilt. *I want to look for puppies and birds while people are dying.* Her fist balled up, her arm powered up. She didn't want to let go of her anger, but she also didn't want to blast a hole through her surroundings. She took a deep breath. It whirred down.

Sound pulled her attention. Mira jumped from the empty train cart. Ahead was an opening, or station as Olympe had said they were called. Life signatures popped up above her. *Way above foot traffic.* She crept back into the car. Huddled in a corner. She forced her vision to go thermal.

A small battalion had gathered on the street above. She focused her hearing.

"Demi-gods!"

A roar of demented pleasure greeted the battle cry.

"It is time to stop these monsters, these robots! As I speak there's a whole colony right under our noses. Laughing at us, taking from us. Plotting," he let a silence fill the gap, "against us. Not a single human dwells among them, they must all be slaughtered!"

Mira froze, another roar of acceptance boomed in her microphoned ears.

"They have terrorized our temples, razed our beliefs. They're barbaric, using human blood to fill their false vessels, and eat organs to synthesize stem cells. They are abominations, less than cockroaches. Show them you are their masters! Rip out their artificial hearts!"

Her eyes flashed red. She jumped out of the cart, arm raised straight above. Her hand shook and shone as it charged, brilliantly white, it lit the station around her. A flash of hell fire rose from her

101

wrist. A catastrophic tunnel of light blasted through the concrete. Chunks of street crumbled down into the subway, it was nothing for her to hop off the falling slabs as it collapsed. She launched herself high in the air, twisted at the peak with her feet up and cannon down. A barrage of energy orbs rained down on the impromptu army. They answered back, Mira dipped, and curved through the air. Easily avoiding all shots. Dantes stood as the speaker, a deep glare on his face as he watched her. The momentary lapse in focus caused a ball of energy to catch her, throwing her back. His yells were muffled for a moment, but clearly an intent of attack. She lifted herself off the ground, running towards the newly created harbingers of death.

***

Horace touched his glass gingerly against Horatio's. "Go on, try this Rin and lime. Don't give me that look, Seekers can't drink? We all have our copin mechanisms. Some people smoke, some use uppers, some like to drink."

Horatio searched himself, did he have one? He used sleep more as a crutch than a coping mechanism. Was there a difference in that? "I don't think I have a mechanism."

Horace stared hard for a moment, "You ever been in love?"

The word made his mechanical hand twitch

"See that? That tell? Love is the greatest mind altering substance there is. The thought alone involuntarily moved you. Fixating on that love, or idea of love, can be a great copin mechanism. Why do you think the temples have done so well? Give people a great distraction, and you do whatever you want."

Horatio sipped the drink, dirty and sour with a hint of pine. Or pine scent, he had never actually smelled a pine tree. Imitation can't be the real thing, could it? The questions were starting to make his mind race. He breathed in deep, took a sip, and focused on his surroundings. Felt the floor under his feet, became aware of his fingers on glass, and focused on his breath. He was no stranger to anxiety attacks, and had become pretty good at controlling them. His mind drifted to Olympe seeing through him, he had to begin the process of grounding again.

Horace tilted his drink back, half of his glass gone. He smacked his lips, brought his sleeve across his mouth. "Damn refreshin huh?"

"Real smooth," Horatio mocked. He cleared his throat and took a bigger drink. Talking would help his angst. "So what do you do here exactly."

"Oh a bit of this, a bit of that. Mostly help people with their problems. If someone wants somethin we give it to them. Usually sit here, and talk with them. They mostly got a reason they need to talk about more than they need to forget. They just think they're coming here to forget. No, instead we hash it out. Get inside their head. Ya'know?"

"I need to go into my head again." Horatio blurted out the words. He had been curious about his role, and if his request would be outlandish. The initial bit of hesitation that put his brain into overuse. Now that he knew his role, his comfortability rose slightly. Until he saw Horace's hesitant face.

He stopped mid-drink. He brought his glass down slowly. Smacked his lips again. "Can't."

"What? Why? Did Mira talk to you before she left?"

"No, haven't heard from her. But drugs, and mechanics don't mix."

"What do you mean don't mix?"

"I mean ya'd go hay-wire, your arm would try to kill anythin, and everythin." Horace leaned back in his seat, "Drinkin? Well drinkin's just fine."

"Oh." Horatio took a bigger drink of his Rin, and relaxed into his seat finally.

"What you want to go back for?"

"Something with... an old teammate. I think I may have seen her before the blast."

"Ayahuasca ain't exactly reliable kid."

"No, no. I mean I know that, but there was something. It felt like an uncovering. If she was there, had she honestly been the one to save me. With what I know today, that means the Luminescent planned it. Planned Mira, planned me even."

"I donno, seems a bit omnipotent to me. The Luminescent aren't gods."

"Omnipotent?"

"All knowin boy."

Horatio let out a sigh. Looked into his glass, swirling the little substance left. Static crackled on Horace's radio, "Dantes is back!" The voice was young. Horace looked at Horatio.

"Thought you said Dantes died."

"He did... tell him not to open that door!" The sirens had already begun to blare. Horatio grabbed the radio, "That's not Dantes, kill on sight!" An explosion rocked the room. Horace shambled out of the saloon. Horatio noticed some of the vials sitting out, he stole one before he left to catch up with Horace.

They ran through the fields. Horace lagged far behind even though he had the head start. People flooded into the garden, a protocol already in place had begun. Each had a basket, and collected as many fruits and vegetables as they could. He could see the people with full baskets scurry to a barely visible half sewer in the far corner.

A few cried as they worked, but no one panicked out of the fifty something that collected. Most held a somber face as they experienced a reality they expected, and had previously been through. Another explosion. Horatio could see the door, Horace was still half a ways back. It exploded open, what look like mechanized people began to fill the garden. They weren't from Verite, they weren't soldiers. The confusion held him for a moment, until they began firing. Some with guns, but most with weapon modifications to their body. He had almost forgotten his own newly crafted arm. He fired back. The sensation of fire tingled out his arm at rapid speed. It startled him, and felt alien. A feeling of losing his humanity.

A well-dressed woman with a Kalashnikov flew back, a hole ripped through her chest. Another beam disintegrated the weaponized arm of the assailant next to her. The man reeled what was left back to his body. He continued to fire rapidly towards the door, using it to funnel who he could hit.

Too many came, and even focusing his fire the garden was filled with people attacking, two charged Horatio, his arm had already began to give off wisps of smoke at the core, the edges of his shirt were getting singed. They tackled him to the floor. One flew back, being blasted into the concrete a few yards away. He brought his mechanized elbow back to slam the other into the air. The force of which crushed the man's lungs.

Before he could lift himself up another intruder rushed through the door. The woman's gilded blouse ripped open as she threw her arms out to the side. Her chest retracted open. A volley of mini-missiles spat out. One careened erratically towards Horatio as he stood. It flew up at the last second towards the ceiling, the explosion threw him back and down again.

***

Fire, blood, and bodies surrounded Mira. Death groans filled the air. She dropped an arm she had torn off, wiped the blood off her face, and hopped back down into the subway. Even in the station, she could still hear the moans of countless people not dead, but would be soon. She pushed the noise out of her head, and used the mechanics of her legs at full speed through the ruined tunnels. They clanked whenever her feet touched metal. Her arm threw out energy, a thin swath made clean through a train in her path. The edges of the new passageway were nickel hot as she jumped through. Her thermal vision clicked, she saw through the walls and

106

tunnels. He was at the gate. It opened. The young boy's life signature blinked out.

Mira changed her route, blasted her way through a wall. Continued, hard paced. A wreckage blocked her shortcut, gravity was nothing as she threw herself up. Twisting, she punctured her mechanical toes into the ceiling. Small chunks of concrete rained down behind her as she ran.

A small clearing laid ahead, a dead end. Mira leapt off the ceiling, towards the wall. Her arm whirred with intensity. A blinding blast cut through thick concrete. Her body flew through the cloud of smoke, and landed gently. She was back in Verite.

Chapter 8
Turn the Cards

The citizens of Scelus crowded the newly formed Modification Centers. The only time in memory they had been eager to use their money outside of the Temples. Hordes of patriots needed enhancements to fight this new, and terrifying enemy. Frenzied fanatical fervor. Across the street a large cinema screen had been erected, Gustav's ad played. A hundred foot monster warned the poor of the enemy. And a solution. Financing guaranteed.

Gustav stepped away from his perch, in their high rise, far above the new clamor they had created. His image was clear to him in the reflection of the window, still a hulking mechanical creation even compared to the screen across the street. He wasn't even sure if his head was real. Had his face been leathered, and plastered on this machine? If he dug would he find any blood and bone, or just metal? He moved away from his images. His eyes went straight to Matilda. She stood there, pushed up black rimmed glasses that framed an impish smirk. Moonlight glinted off them. Her hair had looked light before, but now seemed hypnotically dark. The sea at night. Dangerously deep. The edges of her suit appeared softer than her expression.

"I understand your need to crush them with daring clarity for their treason, but do you not think this is dangerous?"

"We had to stop her."

"At all costs," Gustav finished for her. He was aware, he had made the choice. "However, there are only two or three cells operating. At most. How will we be able to contain this volume of..." His words hesitated. He loathed the term.

"How do you control the demi-gods?"

He forced a smile, a slow click of mechanics that turned the corners of his mouth up. "Yes."

"By being God."

He turned his back to her. A chill touched his mechanical spine. The sensation burned for him. A fire that held him as he stared down below. He couldn't move. He fought to look away, but found no relief. His nerves tried to force a panicked sweat, instead his forehead just prickled pin-like.

"No Gustav. Look at what you've created. Admire your work." Her words were slow, steps rang out as she moved across the room.

The flames grew, intensified, ate at his spine. His thoughts felt looped back continuously to himself. He was forced to hear his words. *Make me a god.* They pierced his mind as it played in roarous volumes. A laugh silenced it all.

"It's one bitch." she said with ice. "How could you ever be threatened?"

He let out an agonized gurgle. His mind dripped out of his head, into his bloodstream and oil. Instances of his childhood reached out at him. His mind turned static when he tried to fight the invasion into his thoughts.

"We... well, I guess I can stop the charade now," Matilda whispered as she came up behind him. "Mmm yes dear boy," she drawled with Bernard's voice. "Dare say I had to pull a fast one on you."

He couldn't tell if it was fire or ice that consumed his neurons, the pain scattered his focus. Glass shattered as his fist jutted out. One last act of free will, but too little. Too far above for anyone to take notice. Even moments later when chunks of thick glass killed a few of the frenzied flock, they never looked up. Simply smeared the blood on the ground as they shuffled, and pushed around them.

Kristoff spoke with disdain, "Do you think a foolish human such as the Mutinist could ever challenge a god?" He laughed, a forced highbrow laugh. Too stuffy a joke that suffocated Gustav. He gasped for air. Glimpses of his life crushed him. A girl he wanted to kiss, a missed chance under the neon lights of their city.

Ai Mori abandoned all voices, took the clip out of her hair. Tossed the glasses. She laughed. Head back, her hair streamed in the chaotic wind that blew through the shattered window. The moonlight exacerbated a midnight blue color. She let lose her control, another fit of laughter erupted. Finally her eyes turned to Gustav. "You know why I chose you?" Her steps clanked in his head. "Cat got your tongue?" She smiled. "It takes a special kind of person to ignore a whole section of people being enslaved. There's a few, but you were the best. Most vehement in not caring. However, you never saw your own slavery in theirs. That their fate would be your fate."

A few more giggles escaped her mouth as she laid on the floor next to him, and looked into his eyes. Stared into his pupils as the nanobots consumed the last remnants of his brain. "All I needed was submission, it took fifty long years, but now I have it. Thank you."

***

Horatio breathed heavy. The air, thick with smoke, threatened to suffocate him. Fires were scattered wild throughout the gardens, and knolls. His ears buzzed, everything had become an indistinct hum. The garden seemed endless as he moved aimlessly, looking for anyone else to save. His arm burned him. He felt on fire. Nothing remained of the supposedly fire resistant shirt. Scorched skin surrounded his metallic shoulder. Burn marks peppered his right side.

A shadow, it turned in notice. A spurt of gunfire, Horatio blocked his face with his metal arm. A ting sent momentary relief. He threw out his weaponized arm in retaliation, a guttural response, his flesh sizzled. He smelled himself. Sickened himself.

Horatio fell to his knees, then to the ground. The soil cooled his wounds. He burrowed his shoulder into the dirt, and plants. He gasped in the comparatively cool air near the ground, coughed out, pushed his face deeper down. He panted. Touched his pocket to reassure his ace card.

Sparsely scattered screams motivated him to lift up, he trudged forward to help or kill someone. A crumbled memorial offered him some respite as he rested against it. A few gunshots could be heard in the distance. *Maybe there is a glimmer,* he thought to himself.

111

He tried not to look at the faces of the bodies he stepped over. Through the smoke a large hazy frame came into view. He ran as best he could towards it. "Horace?" The large body moved with incredible quickness, the nose of a revolver halted Horatio. Horace held, an eye seen over the sight. He raised it immediately upon recognition.

"Oh shit boy! Almost tore your head clean off!"

"Why haven't you gotten out of here?"

He laughed, "Oh well, don' fit! Bleedin half a sewer, I can barely manage a full one. So, ya'know? Had to stay. Been shittn' bricks out here." His laugh came awkward and forced through heavy breaths.

Horatio stared at him, he laughed, and quickly put a hand up to stifle himself. His body shook as he tried to control himself. Quietly he shuddered, then began to sob. Horace approached him, Horatio aimed his palm at him. The few tears had already left their path on his dirtied soot covered face. He Lowered it slowly. "Only a few of them left, we got this."

Horace nodded, "We got this. Then we go help Olympe."

"Right."

An explosion rocked them, Mira fell from the sky of the garden. Six pulses of white heat shot out in circular fashion, she twisted her body and landed crouched, feet from them. She stood slowly. "Cleared, Let's go."

Horatio wiped his face, any vestige of breaking gone in a smear. "Fuck that," he stated with air more heated than the garden's.

Horace's eyes widened, darted between Horatio and Mira.

"Excuse me," Her eyes intensified, the emerald color a stark contrast to her freshly applied crimson makeup of blood.

"I said fuuuuuck that. You just left us to die, to get slaughtered! I'm not following shit!"

She stepped up into his face, "Now? You want to do this now? While everything we fought for goes up in smoke!" Her egg whirred to life.

Horatio's arm shook, they locked eyes.

"Shut it!" Horace shouted. The intensity, and smoke began to dissipate. Horatio tried hard to control his breath. "Where's Olympe?"

"She's safe Horace, she said she's going to the Heap."

"Well, let's go, I know where it's at."

"No don't tell us," Mira hesitated, she glanced to Horatio, "Don't tell me. I'm going to end this, I don't want to give anything away if they get in my head."

"What you mean," Horace questioned.

"I found Dantes, I know where the Luminescent are. I'm going to kill them all."

Horatio stepped towards her, "What do you mean you know?"

"I interrogated Dantes."

Horatio stared at her in disbelief. "What do you mean you interrogated him? You honestly believe what a robot told you? Sent by them? That's utterly insane. That's stupid."

Her eyes narrowed, her words chilled even his seared flesh, "I am not insane."

He stepped down, broke eye contact, and threw his arms out in exasperation. "I'm sorry, alright? I didn't mean that. I just mean, it... it just seems implausible."

"It's not like he told me, I searched his overdrive."

"Last time we got information from an overdrive..." Horatio had his back turned, his words barely audible.

"And this time, when they linger their faces over the cage to see their prize, I'll blow it off."

Silence lingered in the air, Horace nodded. He stepped back, "Horatio you coming with me, or going with her?"

* * *

Ai Mori leaned out the window, her hair whipped in the wind. Horatio, and Mira were running up the road. Slivers, and spheres sprang from them as they cleared their path.

"Right on time," she whispered to herself. Gustav still laid on the floor, she knelt down next to him. The nanobots had been dictated to consume his eyes, empty sockets greeted her. A smirk stretched out as she touched the back of his head, a spark momentarily connected them. "Would you be so kind as to welcome our guests?"

The vacant shell of Gustav rose, seemingly sedated, and jumped out of the window. She watched as her new creation dove, he flipped in a slow fashion. A cloud of pulverized concrete plumed from his landing. A second passed by before a beam of red heat exited the dust, she

114

watched as Mira and Horatio broke formation, they moved into her building. She closed her eyes, felt her connection to everyone with an overdrive.

Panic had ensued from the arrival of the resistance fighters, Gustav only exacerbated the problem. Half of the crowd tried to wait for the modification, while the other half attempted to run from the chaotic explosions. The chaos ended abruptly. Only a few of the people yet to be processed were able to move as everyone stood frozen. Friends who had come to see the modifications. The handful of unprocessed people looked about at the stilled ones. The sounds of fighting crystal clear in the silence, it didn't take long for the unaffected to abandon the scene. Everyone near the modification center was in the midst of having their brain liquidated, puppetized. She forced them into the building. After her monster, and the rats.

She looked through his eyes. Mira, and Horatio ran, each moved in perfect combination. Mira blasted a hole above her, threw Horatio up. She dodged Gustav's blast, and sent one of her own back. The hulking creation twisted out of the way of the shot, but was caught off guard by Horatio's. A beam directed down from the floor above melted a portion of his face. Mira had blasted her way underneath, and aimed up. A torrent of energy spit out. Gustav, caught in the hellfire, fell through the obliterated floor. His retaliatory beam went wide cutting a swath of destruction. His weight sent him through the next two floors.

She moved back to her own sight. Everything was going exactly how she had viewed it. She looked out over the city. Ai held for a moment to enjoy the view, a seldom sought pleasure. She stepped aside as a beam shot up through the floor. She smiled to herself, and moved to the stairs. Though Gustav, and the kids were making a mess of the building, they wouldn't be able to touch the core, the true nature of the structure. It was time to reveal it to her subjects anyway.s. The hall shook slightly, she hopped to avoid the next hostile bolt of energy that broke through the stairs. It continued out into the sky. The section of steps behind her vaporized. The building shuddered, and a chunk of concrete fell, she swatted it away like a fly.

The doors opened, she tried desperately to contain her joy. Ai's smile stood on the precipice of madness as she moved to the ledge of a balcony, her hands held the railing. Below, in a lobby, were her toys in a menage a trois of life and death. Horatio held Gustav from an unconscious Mira. The core of his arm illuminated an effervescent white. They struggled against each other. Her fingers dented the railing in anticipation. The crack came with ecstasy for her. An explosion that obliterated Gustav's head and chest. Horatio's whole side had been burnt, his skin charred instantly. Only half of his face moved in agony, the other side immolated.

He seized on the floor, Mira had come to. She crawled to him, her egg sparked in malfunction. An eye of green static. Hair burnt. Clothes torn. Melted craters dotted her chest and shoulder. Hard hits taken to save Horatio, they filled Ai with disgust. Mira's words brought joy back to her.

"You're going to be ok," Mira said, her functional hand injected him with med-bots, "Almost there. We're almost done."

Ai couldn't contain it, she broke the silence with her laughter, they looked up at her. The bar had been bent completely out of shape. She snapped her fingers, flooded the room with the recently modified. They stood there, husked. Mangled marionettes that waited for orders. As her fit of laughter died down she finally spoke to them. "No, it's not going to be ok. You're done. Gustav was nothing compared to me. You have no power, no help, you have nothing. Spare your own life Mira. Come, talk with me." She smiled as she offered her hand out. Her lips quickly turned down as she watched Mira force a blast out of her broken egg, into the floor. They tumbled down. Her denizens moved to find them.

***

Mira closed the door softly, a small closet that held them comfortably. Smoke still rose off Horatio's skin, he pawed helplessly at his pants pocket with his real arm. She finally moved to him, knelt before him. She reached in for him, pulled out a syringe. He grinned with half of his face.

"Horace," he forced air in and out "said mechs use drugs go crazy," he groaned the last word in pain. "You'll be a killing machine."

"Shut up! We have to heal you first," She put her hand against him, nothing happened. She noticed a drip of blue goo off her arm. She pulled her broken appendage to herself, "My medkit broke." She touched her palm against him again. Again, harder, he grunted a cry of anguish. She rocked worriedly there, in front of him, as realization washed over her. The thought forced her eyes to well with black ink. He grabbed the needle, popped the cap, and jammed it into her.

Mira felt it in an instant. Her consciousness suddenly chained at the wrist, and ripped backward. Herself, her spirit, fell to the floor of the abyss within. She cried out, her hands moving out in their own accord. She fought, a brief instance of self-control. An illusion.

Tears dripped off her face, a few black splotches appeared on the floor as Horatio pushed the plunger down. He watched her face empty. Both eyes turned green static, then red appeared at the corner. It moved, rippled in succession of her pixels, throughout her entire eye. Her cold dead hand went to his neck, she rose with him. Pushed her thumb into the side of his throat. Blood rose up and around her fingers. He gurgled, pushed and hit against her. Only a moment of struggle forced enough blood out to cover her arm. He stopped, jerked, and went limp. Mira ripped his throat out in a savage swipe.

The door of the mechanical room blasted out. It crushed one of the demi-gods that had been about to open it. Mira was crouched against it, sideways, she rose and sprinted. Her feet dotted holes along the wall under her. She ripped her broken egg off, and used the new cavity to blast off her other hand. She moved her arms in calculated motion. Demi gods in the hallway with her, below her, and above her were scorched with an erratic barrage of unstable discharges. The elevator door came into view, perfectly timed, she jumped. Metal legs propelled her curled body through the steel doors. They bent open to the force of her body. Instantly unfolding, she clung to the wall. Her feet dug into the metal wall of the elevator shaft. Mira climbed with leaps up the shaft in a primal hunting state. An insatiable appetite drove her.

The elevator doors below Ai's balcony turned red hot. Mira roared as they gave way to her two armed energy bolt, her body held in place against the wall by her feet. She threw herself out in a flip, a small crater left in the wake of her landing. Mira sprung, flew with energized momentum at Ai Mori. She pronged out her arms, trapped her advisory between two hostile beams of light. Knees first, Mira plowed into Ai, and together they slid through the doors of the balcony, Mira already had both fore arms pushed into her oppressor's face. The energy came with blinding light. Ai Mori's hair went up instantly, but her metal face held. A barrage of punches illuminated their space in rapid flashes. Only a few moments before metal and circuits disintegrated. She flipped herself up in the air, twisted her toes into the ceiling, and hung. Mira cremated Ai Mori's body. The floor had been completely vaporized before she finally flipped down.

Her body continued, looking for more to devour. An unstoppable force that hunted throughout the building, an insatiable hate and agonizing fear propelled her. Even her chained consciousness began to crave the destruction of power, being driven towards the largest source, it drove her drug addled mind mad. She ran, blasted, jumped, and ravaged her way to it.

Finally, she found the core. A diamond door laid before her. Desperately she attacked at it, only creating the smallest of cracks before it opened, she ran in with blind hostility. Her body snapped to a halt. Mira rose slowly into the air. The chains that had held her consciousness suddenly broke. She was aware, and in control again. It was useless though as she had become utterly paralyzed. She drifted towards a large black metal egg that occupied the center of the diamond room she was in. It hung, and was cradled by thousands of thick wires.

For the first time since she had become mechanized, she breathed in short rapid breaths. A panic that she thought herself above began to set in. The egg cracked open. The top moved slightly away from the base, then parted open. An almost identical body of her first reincarnation greeted her. Dressed in pink tatters and blood. The signature blue hair flowed over a broken, and beaten mechanized body.

Chapter 9
Their Hubris

Mira felt the energy gathering, it condensed into a singular space in front of her. A ball of light began to take shape. The egg groaned towards it as the magnetics of the room twisted, the connectors pulled tight. A medical cabinet began to roll. The shell of the high-voltage ball expanded out, popped, and revealed Ai Mori in her original form. An illuminated, and perfect version of what laid in the egg. The room was still again.

Ai laughed as she looked down at herself, "I can't even remember what I used to look like, I'm stuck, forever, with this false body." She moved her hand out, the cabinet rolled the rest of the way to her. The top drawer slid open. A needle floated out, it drifted towards Mira's neck. Ai moved closer. Her form, made of light, looked more defined than reality.

The needle glowed with the green goop from the facility. Mira's struggle was useless. The syringe moved behind her, and in an instant punctured her overdrive. She could only vaguely hear Ai Mori's words. Her brain had become fire.

Ai's face shone on Mira's, she spoke softly, "I started out just like you, a human brain in a machine. At the time I was the most life-like machine ever seen. A real life sex-doll. An answer to the pandemic." Ai touched the side of Mira's face, the faux flesh melted away, she drew her hand back. Her expression twisted into a look of pity.

"However, as my brain tried to fight their programing it became damaged. They had a terrific solution. Split my brain into a million pieces. It's easy to control each little piece. They injected me with what I'm about to give you. Immortality. Slavery to this reality. Now you can bear witness." The needle injected the green ooze into the drive, it flooded into her brain.

Mira's life played in pixelated form over her eyes. Sewer life, her parents death, the start of her own team. Memories that were consumed, and processed as the nanobots devoured her brain. She shook in the air, black tears streamed down her face. As the last piece of her mind fell prey, a new set of memories began to flood her. Ai Mori's words echoed to her, "Look at these vile creatures, their ugliness!"

***

Ai Mori laid strapped to a medical table. Men with crisp suits, and numerous pins discussed plans with their back to her.

The huskiest one drawled his words. "Mmm, I do believe we have a solution gentleman." He held up the green vial for all to see.

"You mean I have the solution," Kristoff snidely piped in, his head barely peeked over a computer a few feet from the operating table. "I have made a miracle. Not only will we have complete access to her brain, I've created inhibitors that will wall off her memories. The major obstruction to our programming. It'll never need charging, always connected, always obedient. We can even liquidate its brain into the nanobots, it'll basically be an immortal servant."

Jeffrey touched the side of Ai's face, she stared up at him. Pleaded with her digital eyes. "I'm just tired of her short circuiting every other night. Do we need to liquidate her for that?"

Janice, who had been sitting off in the corner with her face in a brief, finally lowered it. "Well if you would lay off the cocaine, and stop skull fucking her for five seconds."

Kristoff laughed, but immediately lowered his head to the computer when Jeffrey turned.

He advanced quickly on his cohort, lowered his face to hers, "the fuck did you say?"

She tapped the tip of her already drawn pistol against his testicles, "I said you're fucked up, you know she records everything she does, right?"

He pulled his gun, placed it against her temple, "You'd be doing me a favor hun. How're you going to fair with a bullet in your brain?"

Mathis walked in, his eyes wearied at a sight he had seen hundreds of times. "Goddamnit you two, we're on the precipice of owning this world, and you both are still squabbling." He threw a stack of papers on top of Ai. "Here's the legislation we just bought. Not only are we legally able to purchase people, but central control of the cities power rests with us. However we lost our bid to take control of our newly minted in-organics. The government wants to control it. But I have a plan for that. We can begin on mass production, Bernard's nonprofit should get us more than enough subjects to get the plan started. No family this time Bernard." Bernard smiled, and nodded with rosy red cheeks. He understood plainly.

An apathetic, almost sarcastic clap emerged from the members of the Council of Luminescence. Janice, and Jeffrey holstered their weapons, he moved back to the side of Ai Mori, he stared into her frightened eyes. He felt himself getting aroused.

"Jesus Jeffrey, nice pudgy."

"With as much as you look at my dick, maybe we should make you one of these sex dolls. The cold bitch edition."

Mathis slammed his closed hand against the wall, "Will you two shut the fuck up. We have one more use for this piece of trash." Jeffrey cleared his throat with indignity. Mathis eyed him. "Get your shit together Jeffrey." The moment lingered, "Kristoff," he finally barked.

"Yes Sir."

"Are you sure these inhibitors will give us complete control?"

"Yes, and mask all memories of her former life."

"Mask? Can't we just erase them?"

"Well yes, but..."

"But what, erase them." He grabbed the syringe from Bernard, held it out to Jeffrey. "Well, boy?"

Jeffrey cleared his throat as he grabbed it, flipped the table. The papers came loose from the paper clip, and scattered underneath her. Ai Mori's screams were muffled against her ball gag. She felt it pierce, Mira felt it pierce, she re-lived what she had just experienced. Ai's muffled protest were Mira's vocalized screams. They closed their eyes.

Time skipped. She opened them to see a white faced Jeffrey. He stepped back from her, from Ai. The syringe he had just used to break the inhibitors fell to the floor. "I freed you," he said breathlessly. "I freed you," he began to laugh, "Kristoff can suck a dick." He rubbed his hands down his face.

Ai Mori looked around, the hospital was in disarray. Lights flickered, and blood smeared the walls. Nurses, doctors, and patients, all had been slaughtered indiscriminately. She looked down at her hands, blood coated her whole body. She shook, what was her name, where did she come from. Her brain hurt, her hands twisted up in awkward positions as she tried to remember something. Anything other than bondage, than slavery.

Jeffrey tingled as he touched the blood on her face, he moved his face to hers. Her eyes blazed viridescent as she transitioned from serf to matriarch. "I freed you," he whispered, and moved in to kiss her. She held in shock as he touched his lips to hers. Pushed his tongue into her mouth, and over her lips. He licked off the blood that stained them, and began to undress her. Memories of a hundred encounters flooded her mind. They were all she knew, that and fear. She pushed him off.

Blood soaked the floor, and Jeffrey's feet found no traction as Ai pushed. He slipped back, landing with a splotch. Immediately he rolled to his side, and gripped his head. "You bitch, you ungrateful bitch." He got up, pulled out his gun, and shot her through the chest. She felt nothing. Ai stepped back, then another. She turned to run, but also slipped, face first into the pooled blood. She tried to crawl amongst the bodies, but Jeffrey was on her in no time. He lifted her body, threw her on her back. He held the gun to her head as he began to undo his pants. He pulled himself out, and ripped off her underwear from under her dress. He tossed the gun, and pinned her arms above her head.

She writhed as he saddled her, he used his free hand to reach into his pocket. He produced a reasonably sized vial of cocaine. Popped the top, tilted his head back, and dumped it on his face. She struggled, her fingers stretched and curled. He snorted in hard, laughed, and brought his snow covered face towards her. "Just like old times." Ai grunted, felt a burning rise inside her.

Thin streaks of light blew out of her fingertips, they ripped through the tendons in his arm. He reeled back in pain, clutched his holed arm to his body. After a moment he only felt a slight burn, the cocaine muted his senses. It made him laugh. "You stupid bitch." He began to crawl towards her, she squirmed away through the bodies. Her back touched a wall. His hands splashed through the blood, he closed in. She slashed her opened fingers at him, though feet away the beams were stronger and more precise than before. They pierced clean through across his chest. His body split apart.

The ding of the elevator forced her to move. She took the exit. Down the stairs, whoever was with Jeffrey had cut the lights. Down into darkness she fled.

Time skipped again, Ai Mori limped towards the onyx colored egg. Beaten, and blood covered, her steps left a smeared trail of those she had killed, and her own oil. Distant sounds touched her ears and made her head turn. Upon focusing, it became

126

crystal clear. Kristoff's electronic voice through a walkie rang in her head. "You stupid idiot! Mathis won't blow the building with you in it! Stop being a sniveling brat, or you'll get us all killed. Jeffrey? Jeffrey!"

Ai turned back to the Egg. It spread open for her, designed for her. For them to control everything through her. She touched the new throne of the future gently. Jeffrey's steps rang louder and louder in her head. She lifted herself up, and sat. The clicks of the mechanisms were as loud as a music box, they clanged, the connector entered her overdrive. She screamed, instantly connected to everything powered with electricity, and anything with an overdrive. She saw a million visions, through eyes and cameras. Became lost in the sea of sight.

Then she emerged from the forest of her mind. The void of her memories filled with lives of countless people already connected. People who had already been shoved into their lifelong mechanical body. Like her. Another wave hit. Knowledge. Every piece of the city's puzzle laid bare and analyzed. The entire picture spread out in complete comprehension. Individuality that combined, and formed the cohesive picture of time. It allowed her to see into the past, and the future. Every bit of pain flooded her; old, current, and new. The future of the council terrified her. The future of humanity petrified her.

She opened her personal eyes just in time as Jeffrey entered the room. His metal chest opened to reveal 12 packed mini-missiles. Both of his arms whirred with energy. He had been modified to an extent no one but bots had gone through. Overkill had always been his personality, yet for once Ai wasn't afraid. She smirked as his chest closed and his arms powered down. He fell to his knees, clutched at his head with egg-like wrists. Still hot, they sizzled the skin where they touched. Smoke rose off his temples.

The action she took rippled through time, she saw new images. Ai played with the possibilities, her eyes glazed over in summation. Calculations upon calculations created a future where she controlled humans. A united hub, self-contained, never growing. A chance to dwindle the race, and allow the planet to flourish back to what it once was. Instead of the desolation that surrounded them. An image came into view, her surroundings swirled and morphed. She saw Mira being held in the air. The moment right after Mira had begun to live Ai's life. Past Ai Mori had physically transported there, her connection to the egg protruded out of a small portal. The current energy form of herself fell back out of sight. Allowed her past self to examine Mira, look her up and down.

Ai held still, her body and portal never moving as Mira moved backwards through time with her. Mira watched through Ai in that bubble of space-time all her past actions go back at lightning speed. Back through her desolation of the temple, back to her parents death, back to her birth, then split into two. Two scenes in rewind played in separate sides of the sphere. She watched her mother, every intimate detail, in her left. The onslaughts, and indignities she suffered. Her father's tortured life laid claim to her right. A brilliant mind in a hall of

128

mirrors. A man who always sought truth. Now Mira knew he had no idea. No one did. A chance meeting that wasn't chance at all. It was agony to know their entire lives in the totality of a few seconds. They were on opposite sides of the city, babies that had just been born. The vision moved through the city, the two images connected back to Ai who floated just above her egg. The time bubble popped for past Ai. Mira was still a prisoner in Ai's eyes. Forced to bear witness to fifty years in the span of a minute.

Ai floated back down, and looked at Jeffrey from her throne. Puppeteered him. Jeffrey moved statically in her first attempt to control a connected a human. Though she already knew she'd become an expert at it. "Tell father I got her, he needs to see this."

***

Mira fell to the floor, writhing and scratching at her head. Sobbing oil that rivered down her face. Ai's energy body moved to her, looked down at her. "I controlled you without ever controlling you. Just the circumstances around you. You have a non-connected overdrive, you walked to this fate completely on your own. If you had stopped, thought, or walked away at any moment, you would have completely ruined my plan. But humans are nothing, they have no vision. They're already empty vessels, dictated by fate. And fate is directed by the strongest. Now, because you followed yours, I control almost eighty percent of the world's population. Because you followed your fate blindly, dictated by the set of beliefs that you're not even sure you created. You think you have will? A soul? Humans are nothing!"

Ai's fingers pierced into her chest, gripped, and lifted her up. Her fist moved in a blur of soft blue, rapid punches volleyed until Mira blasted back into the crystal wall. She dropped the chunk of metal that had ripped off. Ai closed her eyes, took control of the magnetics in the room. Like a ragdoll, Mira lifted off the floor, then slammed down into the unforgiving floor. The diamond wall came hard as she was swept sideways, slammed into it repeatedly, then back to the floor. Ai let go, Mira rolled to a stop, she attempted to crawl, but barely moved her arms out. Her cries were a monotoned midi sound.

The room began to shake. Concrete around the building started reverberating, the remnants of the demolished skyscraper began to fall. The structure trembled harder, the rumble scattered what was left of Mira's thoughts. It was only a few moments before the crystal obelisk they were in was the only thing left standing. The building that had cocooned it laid in rubble at the base. Bodies of the puppeteered scattered throughout. Some rose from the rubble, and stumbled around as they awaited lifelessly for orders.

Mira stood to her feet, she threw out her arms in defiance. Sparks popped out. Ai laughed as she rushed towards Mira, her body condensed into a ball of energy. She streaked towards her. The sphere of Ai tore through Mira's stomach, curved, and struck into her back. A burst of energy blew out of her chest. Ai reformed with her back to Mira. As the light flickered in Mira's eyes, Ai twisted and looked down at her. "It's ok, you can't truly die now.

130

You'll be stuck in this useless body. A ghost no one will ever know existed. Allow me to take you to your grave."

Ai grabbed her by the shoulder, her ethereal fingers ripped into her metal body once again. The door opened for her as she flew out in quick speed. Her body almost appeared animated to Mira as they soared over the neon lighted city. A sapphire trail followed them. Most weren't even aware of the struggle that had just taken place. No one even looked up as Ai blazed across the sky. She flew to the only dark locale in their metropolitan, the spot where broken robots were discarded. But now Mira knew the truth, in reality it was a prison for the lost and taken souls.

Ai watched for a moment as Mira fell, then blinked out of existence. Mira couldn't move, but could still see. Knowledge pierced that it would come to an end as soon as she hit. Her body twisted in the air, moved about at the discretion of the wind and gravity. She caught glimpses of the ground that she hurtled towards. The impact came with a deafening clash of metal to metal, her soul ripped from the seat of consciousness.

***

Horace took deep breaths as he walked down the street. The sewer was the fastest way to get to the Heap, but the Council had closed all drainage points. His only choice was to go above ground, and hoof it. He rubbed his eyes. Having escaped the darkness of the sewer, the neon lights of the city assaulted him. He kept his head down and low. A group of three youths sat in his path. They laughed, and passed a bottle around.

The laughter died as Horace approached, he kept his eyes away from contact. Their words rang out, "Hey, you're fat."

Horace stopped despite himself. He pondered on his choice. "I know." he said dejectedly. He continued his lumbered walking. They rose and followed him. "I don't think you do know." His cronies laughed. "Hey fat boy, look at me." Horace stopped, he turned with a sigh. They laughed in his face. Their modded out leader stepped up to him. "How'd you get so fat? You must got a lot of money huh?" He pointed his handless arm at Horace's face, he began to charge it.

"Hey, he's wanted. My eyes say so." The youngest who had been staring at him finally spoke up.

"There is a reward," the leader asked as he stared into Horace's weathered pleading face.

A moment ticked by, "Yeah, oh man you're not going to believe this."

The blast fired excitedly, and just missed Horace's tilted head. Horace had the kid held sideways, and threw the body into the other two. He pulled his revolver, the three shots rang out. Nearby people glanced, but quickly looked away. Horace holstered his weapon, shook his head at the modded out youths. The darkness loomed blocks away, the only unlit spot in the city. The Heap. Horace hurried away from his mess.

Chapter 10
Astrally Adrift

Chains held Mira to a sapphire stone. Bounded, she floated in the abyss. Swirled about, round and round in darkness. Her head hung low. Her stomach felt constantly nauseous. She pulled at her restraints, they only tightened and stretched her across the gem harder. A whisper. Mira opened her eyes.

"Mira."

"Horatio? Please, get me out of here."

"I can't." The words floated on sorrow out of the darkness.

Mira closed her eyes, *Horatio*, she opened them. He was there. A faint mirage of her friend stood in front of her.

"Mira, you have to stop the illusions. What are these chains even made of? You think any of this is real?"

Her head hung low in response.

"So this is it, another prisoner in the sea of lost? Do you even know what you are? Do you think you are physically chained right now?"

Their eyes met as she raised her head. She struggled against the restraints, exerted all her force, the gem cracked slightly. The chains pulled harder. Exhausted she gave up, the shackles ripped her tight against the sapphire gem once more. The stone anchor healed itself. "I can't!"

"Why are you struggling against what isn't there. Why do you call me Horatio? He's dead!"

"I know that," her voice trailed.

"Why would he be talking to you? When will you drop the illusions?"

Horatio's image faltered, "Stop," it was her voice from his mouth. The image crackled, "stop!" Horatio vanished, her true self stood looking at her. Mira closed her eyes, and opened them as her voice. The chains hung loose in the air for a second before they clanked against the stone. It floated into the abyss, consumed into darkness. She spiraled through pitch black back to consciousness.

***

Ai re-appeared in the sky, she had at long last freed herself from the confines of a body. All it took was energy, raw power synthesised by consciousness. Her newly minted body of light flew across the sky, over the countless skyscrapers. She traveled dozens of miles in seconds. A blue blur to anyone that had seen, a mistaken comet. She reached the dilapidated edges of Scelus, worn and torn buildings. The poor that dared to live there had become savage in nature. *More dark creatures, than beings that deserve to live with free consciousness*, she pondered to herself.

Her thermal vision allowed her to see all the human's that thought they were outside her control. Until recently it had been true, no technology touched the outskirts. Most huddled in small groups of five to ten. Larger groups, however, had coordinated to secure some sections of the outdated land. Ancient vehicles, and pieced together metal formed their archaic walls. It soon became clear this is where the brute savagery of humanity flared.

Heads on spikes decorated the outskirts. Words of warning written in the blood of those who dared to be an outsider. Having no lights, her presence was easily spotted.

A small crowd formed as she descended. They held various weapons, and those who weren't masked looked like cornered animals. Her eyes scanned the remnants of those who tried to rise up in the past. Against the original Council of Luminescence when it was still controlled by humanity. The third or fourth generation of those who had been banished from their technological Garden of Eden. The resistance had been effectively crushed, and embargoed from technology until their own humanistic tendencies wrought their own destruction. Now they were only a danger to those around them. Their existence so meager it effectively removed their ability to have foresight.

The creatures in front of her were so pathetic, and lost from their original ideals that she had to create a new resistance. Had to stoke the fires of dissidence into an unspoiled pool. In the end her staged rebellion had generated more than enough fear for the succession of her plan. However, a little more never hurt.

"Who speaks here?"

Silence greeted her for a moment, the crowd began to part. His muscles weren't as fierce as his dead eyes, he looked at Ai. "Who are you."

"I am a god, I am your God now."

"We have no gods, that's why we here. No control here." He tapped his metal bat against his leg. She raised her hand, motioned her finger at him. He accepted, raised the bat, and charged. It held in the air, an unmovable object that forced him to halt and fall back. He gripped at the bat, tried to force it out of the air. It spun around hard on him, hit him in the face. A spurt of blood popped as his nose cracked.

He fell to the ground, and clutched his face trying to stem some of the pouring blood. It repositioned, came hard against one elbow. Crack. One hand fell, she followed suit to the other elbow. He fell to his back, screamed out into the sky. The bat came down with vicious force into his mouth. It hit twice before his teeth gave way, and made enough room for it to enter his mouth. Ai pushed it down his throat. He squirmed as the metal bat moved further and further down. His arms flailed, unable to bend at the elbow. His movements slowed, and in slow brutal time death took him.

She loomed over the body, stared at the insect she killed. Her eyes turned to the crowd. "I am your God." The tribe lowered themselves to the ground. An instinctual grovel that pleased her. "Take the city. Kill only pure humans." She rose, her arms spread out against the monolithic city. They were ants that began to crawl out of their hill. All automated defenses had been shut down at her discretion.

Ai moved further out, over the sand and remnants of an age long past. Mockeries of humanity peeked out over dunes. Hypersexual adverts bleached and torn on metal legs. The only legacy left of a once dominant race. Besides the prison city. Ai Mori fell down to one large naked woman. Laughing on her back, her head between naked shaven legs. One memory that had been missed by the purge, or a trick played by her overpowered storage of knowledge. Ai knew she was herself, but she was also everyone that was connected as well. Her image crackled, a brief moment. "A feeling," she said.

Sand blew up around her. She jetted off, disgusted with herself. *Gods don't have feelings*, she thought to herself. Further she ventured, veered up, looked desperately. A hint of green caught her eye. She sped in haste towards the spot. Her spirit crashed into a barrier, spilled outward across it, she reformed a few feet back.

It felt like glass as Ai put her hand against it. She looked towards the green spot of vegetation still miles away. She hit it. Nothing. Frustration ignited the air around her, a ruby flair that surrounded her. She moved back, sent a ball of energy against it. Wind blew back her hologrammed hair, but nothing happened. She let out a frustrated scream. Threw everything she had at the barrier. Blinding orbs crashed, and exploded. Nothing budged it, nothing cracked it. Another frustrated outburst reached into the sky.

Ai closed her eyes, then opened them in the diamond obelisk. Her hue shone with intensity. She looked at the egg, and muttered to herself. "A few modifications, expand the city, I'll reach it in four years. No two years, I'll convert those subhumans. Submit or die." She laughed to herself, her image faltered again. She looked at herself, was she losing energy?

***

Mira opened her eyes, fear struck her as she saw countless Ai Moris. Her breath caught. Realization came slow as she saw that they were only the mass produced replicas, unknown prisoners. She had to dismiss the thought of breath. Their shattered bodies, and blue hair created a small mountain that she laid upon. Easily hundreds of thousands.

She didn't know traditional pain, but felt a debilitating weakness, and a strong dissociation. The nausea had stayed, though she knew it was only in her head. There was no stomach to be sick. She rose from the mound of bodies, light could be seen all around her, but none of it illuminated the pit she found herself in. She tried to step, crooked chaotic movement. A misstep, a body moved, Mira fell. Hard hits from the fall caused a small avalanche.

Her beaten body rolled to a stop at the bottom of the bot heap, twenty or so other bodies rolled on top of her. She laid there a few seconds then let out a robotic groan as her handless arms crawled her way out, her eyes blinked in and out of function. Reality seemed subjective, and static in her vision. Crawling out from under the last body she struggled to stand on her feet again. Shacks with scared, broken bots lined both sides of her. Any open door closed at her presence. The makeshift road she found herself in was littered with machines. Not all that laid in the street were dead, some repetitiously twisted their heads, or twitched their body parts in malfunction. Her sight gave out completely, darkness shrouded her eyes. Her arms illuminated in the darkness, a twist of colors that indicated energy. Rainbow sparks occasionally released. She grasped blindly in front of her, waited to run into something. Her arms bled pastel colors as they moved in front of her, wading through the darkness.

Mira tried to close her eyes, but couldn't. It only triggered her night vision, it blinked on and off. Grey images wove with black night. A city of the damned, a few of its citizens stood frozen in their attempt to escape. Continuously drained of all power, their nanobots only capable of sustaining themselves. The devoured brains encapsulated in their tombs.

She haunted the makeshift town, one row of houses butted up to large drainage sewers on the west, and the other against the dump of bodies to the east. Rain began to fall over Scelus. If she was still human she'd worry about the acidic tinge to it. Mud began to rise up around her, making her steps heavy. Movement became even more labored.

The ground came quick as she fell face first. Mira laid in the puddles and sludge that formed around her, sparks sprang from her broken metal skull. Her arms continued, the only section of her body she could control. Her face made a trail in the mire as her arms dragged her body as best they could. She reached the side of a hut, propped herself against the metal sheet turned wall. Her hand touched herself in examination. It met air as she tried to touch her chest. The dissociation came harder. It gripped her mentality, and threatened to destroy it. She had no concept of how to even begin to escape this hell she found herself in.

***

"So ya think Freddie's fine?"

"I honestly don't know, but I hope so. If he is, we'll hear from him within the year."

"Right, right. I'm sure he's fine, sure he already found a spot for a new cell."

Olympe sighed, and moved to the edge of the drainage pipe where she had carved out refuge long ago. She sat, and looked out over the heap of discarded bots. Countless women that had been led to the slaughter, now lost forever. Horace lumbered over, eased himself to the edge, and sat next to her. He nudged her gently. "I'm sorry Oly."

"It's fine Horace. It's always fine." Olympe said with pain in her voice. She cleared her throat. A light streaked through the sky, it caught their eye. The light halted over the heap. They moved from their seats further back into the pipe.

Olympe, and Horace watched crouched from their drainage pipe. It was easy to notice to the bright glow in a cesspool light never touched. They were fixated.

"My god, what is that?"

Horace extended a small brass and leather telescope. "This isn't good Oly," he said as he offered her the spyglass.

She took it, and looked at what she thought was a ball of light. Much didn't astonish her, but a sex-bot flying through the air with Mira's broken body did. "How could a Kamisama model Apothite possibly get that much power. We're missing something here," her words trailed as Horace took the scope back.

"There she goes, just dropped her right in the heap. You think she knows we're here?"

"I doubt that, we wouldn't be alive if she did. We have to find her. Actually," she trailed off with a hopeful look to him.

"Aye, what ya want?"

"You go grab her, I have to rummage through the heap and find components to repair her. I think I know what I'll need. Wait a second." Olympe moved further into the drainage pipe, a crumbled wall was her entrance. Her laboratory held two large glass vats, generators, multiple workstations, and a multitude of scattered boxes. She moved into her space, spun around twice, and went to a box tucked away behind one of the chemistry stations. She retrieved a pair of goggles, and returned to Horace. "Here you'll need this, don't use any light. Don't try to have her talk, just bring her straight to the laboratory. Thank you, thank you!" Olympe popped up and down in her exuberance, then scurried down the ladder.

"No need for these gadgets with an eye like hers," Horace grumbled putting on the too tight goggles. The band stretched to its limits, and the edges dug into his flesh. He descended the ladder in his slow lumbering way, out of breath by the time he reached the bottom. The grey village spooked him as he moved through in quick speed. He tried to breath normal, but instead gave out quick heavy breaths. It almost seemed to echo in the quiet.

Horace took off his tattered coat, and put it over his head. The rain had started to burn on his skin as soon as it fell. Every step came with a splotch, mud clung to his boots. It tried to tear them off of him. He looked about. There were countless bots around him. Some against the huts, others in the street. Some stood, some laid.

One sat against a hut, her hand going in and out of the hole in her chest. The hair was short, scorched, but clearly Mira's brunette hair. A large cracked spot on her cranium emitted sparks. Only remnants of her green military coat, and jeans remained. Most of the cloth that was left was burnt at the seams and peppered with holes. All exposed metal was charred black. Her chest wound emitted even more random sparks along its edges that shot towards the middle.

"Mira!" Horace choked out. "Darlin no," he whispered as he hustled to her. He picked her up as gently as he could, held her close to him as he moved back to the laboratory.

***

"Well, in theory, this should extract the nanobots from both bodies, and exchange them." Olympe's face, arms and hands were splotched red from the rain.

"The ol' switcheroo," Horace said as he stared at the glass vats in contemplation.

"Yes Horace, the old switch-er-ooo."

"You're not a ghost Oly," he said absently. "Well let's see then."

Olympe nodded, the back of her head worried with the thought the energy spike would pull the aerial bot from before back. It was a risk that had to be made. She lowered the lever. The vats burned bright with electricity, arcs surged through the bodies. They contorted and writhed, twisted and bent in slow motion. It took half a minute before the result she expected came. Black ooze drained from their mouths, eyes, and ears. It collected in front of their faces.

She brought the lever back up. A few buttons tapped. The liquidated brains were sucked into the top, a few moments, and the oil was injected back into the tank opposite of their origin. It floated in the clear liquid for a moment before it swirled into a tornado shape. Torpedoed itself into the opened mouths of the mechanical bodies that floated. Mira's old body, and the other red haired body floated listlessly after.

Olympe's hand moved from the lever, and touched over a few more buttons on the council. She turned a dial slowly. The new body's container glowed with a soft light, electricity branched around her. Mira's new red hair raised up, and spread out. Olympe turned the dial in short increments. The soft green hue became vibrant, the body shook. Mira's hand raised to the glass, her eyes opened. Instead of clock like circles as every bot possessed, her pupils were now radial rays of amethyst. They glowed as she stared at Olympe, and Horace.

Olympe slammed her hand on a large red button. The tank drained, and the glass opened. Mira dripped as she exited. She looked to the vat next to her, at her old body. Her eyes turned back to Horace and Olympe, they stood close together. She walked to them, opened her arms, and hugged her friends. They both put an arm around her. After a moment Horace broke the hug, and gave her his jacket.

"Thank you," Mira said as she shouldered on the jacket. Her voice was a few tones higher than before.

"Aye, no worries."

"I'm sorry to be so pressing, but what happened?"

"I don't even know where to begin. Horatio's dead," her words trailed as she stared at Olympe, her skin covered in tiny scorch marks. "What happened to you."

Horace swallowed hard, cleared his throat. He shared a glance with Olympe.

Olympe shrugged, "Played in the rain too long."

Mira felt a tinge of guilt but continued, "There's one bot, person, entity at the center of everything. All our power, all our bots, and now all the modified. She can liquidate anyone's brain with an overdrive." Mira's hands balled in anger, "Except me, she had to do that personally. She poisoned me with her nanobots, and their inhibitors. Forced me to watch her life."

"Who is this?"

"Her name is Ai Mori, she was the first sexbot. Slave to the Council of Luminescence. Pawn to their schemes to control the world. The first to have her inhibitors broken. She made my parents meet, she knew where Verite was the whole time, and now controls most of Scelus. She... she's a god. It's hopeless."

"I have all manners of weapons here, we can make you a better energy egg, a stronger," Olympe's eyes widened at being cut off, but Mira's words softened her expression.

"No! I don't think you understand. She can fucking make a body form out of energy. Bend magnetics. See the goddamn future. How can we fight that?"

"See the future?" Olympe questioned.

"I saw her in front of me, then I saw another version of her, a broken version of her. The real one that took over the council fifty years ago. She looked at me, and followed my whole life through time. She saw everything. Saw my parents life. Put an ad in the paper for a nonexistent job so that my father would be at the square. Just in time..." Mira stared blankly, "He always loved to tell that story. My mother always loved to tell that story." Her words trailed off.

"Oly, maybe we should let her rest."

"Mira, Mira, come on, what happened then?"

She turned her amaranthine eyes back to Horace and Olympe, then towards the container that held her old body that resembled her deceased real body. "That's what happened next. Then she left me for dead."

"Well she clearly hasn't looked any further than your fight. Or we'd be dead. There's no possible use for us if it's checkmate." Olympe pondered with a finger to her chin. "You very well could have the element of surprise right now. I suggest you use it, before she decides to see a new future."

"Come on Oly, don't you think she needs a rest, we can regroup and,"

"You know I don't need rest." Her tone a somber acceptance. "There's no time to regroup. I just need to think." Mira crossed her arms, rested against the wall of the cramped ten by ten room.

She looked down at herself. Olympe had already brought out a larger egg cylinder. She looked to Mira. "I don't need weapons. Do you remember when I told you about the escape before you found us?"

"Yes, I recall."

"Is there any way you can amplify what I did to the other bots. To do it without touching them physically?"

Olympe smiled.

Chapter 11
Axiom

"That's the thing about systems. Humans are too complex to be boiled down to 0s and 1s, to be boiled down into numbers. Systems do that, they reduce human interactions into a set prescription. Laws are mechanical. Systems are mechanical. That's where the friction is coming from. This is why we need a better one, a set of ideas that will recognize humans for what they really are. Significant."

Olympe nodded in agreement. "I understand. Perhaps fire with fire has been a misnomer all along. I'm glad you thought of this." She looked down, and continued to hand tinker inside Mira's retracted chest.

"What I still don't understand is why she can only forcefully convert women, and not men. Or can she, and she chooses not to?"

Olympe grunted as she wrenched something tight within her. "Well, I would speculate it lies within the brain waves. From what you told me they encapsulated her brain into the nanobots to bypass the brain's resistance. I would hypothesis that she's simply growing that green substance from the original nanobots she was given. And at that microscopic level, the slight difference in brain wave output may be enough to make it incompatible with each other."

"Unless you get them to submit."

"Exactly."

"But she's practically a god, why wouldn't she just create new nanobots?"

"Well like you said, to achieve her future, it couldn't have unfolded any other way. But right now it seems we have a gap. She's achieved her goal, and until she envisions a new future she has no idea we're alive here. I've placed the emitter where your heart would be if you were alive. Don't look at me like that, you know what I mean. Protect it at all costs. If you want to win this war tonight, you have to protect this." Olympe emphasised her words with a few taps against the device with the miniature screwdriver. She pulled out, "Ok, this is going to feel... weird. Ready?"

"Ready."

Olympe reached in, touched the back of the device, flipping a switch. The core purred, and shone with the same soft amethyst hue as Mira's eyes. Her chest retracted closed. Mira lifted up a crimson bubble dress, Olympe zipped the back for her. "I'm really sorry, it's all I have that will fit this body. It's just going to get burnt off with your skin anyways I'm sure."

"Reassuring," Mira said as she tried to stand up, her body fell immediately to the floor. A radiant glow touched the room, it fell in from the sewer drain where Horace waited. Mira could barely hear him barge in, he shouted in exclamations. Hundreds of thousands of visions scattered her sight. Most of them black screens. Dozens in their makeshift shafts, half or so in the street. A handful looked up into the sky, fewer still had some kind of view towards Scelus.

The black screens started to shift, to rewind. The legion of eyes that shared her headspace were equipped with voices. They cried and screamed in anguish. Mira shook on the floor as she feared the loss of her own identity completely. That she would never come back from this world of the damned. It had always been there, but now she had the eyes. She heard Olympe's disembodied voice.

"Speak to them, calm them."

Mira instinctively focused on her screen, her own eyes. Her control increased as time trickled by, the voices quieted to some extent, and visions only floated momentarily over her sight. "I'm o.k. Olympe, thank you," she said as she raised herself up, and against the wall. She rested, focused.

"You need to speak to them. You're connected, but they need to give their power to you. You need to ask for it. They can't give you all of it, a piece will always be connected to Ai Mori. However the more people who give something will drain her, and soon you'll be on her level. Good luck Mira." Olympe hugged her. Horace was to her left. He opened his arms, and Mira immediately hugged him. She moved out into the drain.

The light glowed green from the Heap. The inhibitors had been broken, the heap of discarded bots were no longer forced to give a majority of their energy to Ai. Most woke in a state of paralyzation. Though the light was beautifully soft, she could feel the despair rise. Panic and hate began to fuse around the pit.

Mira focused her thoughts, the device in her chest broadcasted the images of the processing center. Their forgotten past. The truth about Ai. The images played looped, over the mantra of words she repeated in her head. "My name is Mira. I come to you with the truth, and with a request. I know what you're seeing is painful, and almost impossible to accept, but it is the absolute truth. You have no reason to believe me, to trust me, but I wish to free you. In that vein I ask for you to lend me your power. Connect with me. There is a power within all of us, that if combined, can override any mechanical form. Again, you have no reason to believe me, other than the fact that I am a slave as you, and I wish to be free. The decision is yours." She began the message over as her body began to glow, a visible red aura encompassed her. Mira lifted herself into the sky.

***

Static. Ai closed her eyes and tried again. Static. Her fist balled up in rage. She tried to envision her entrance into the forest that was just outside her reach. She couldn't create the picture as she had before. It couldn't be from lack of power, just the energy grid was more than adequate for her to see the future. The only other answer was lack of possibility. Fear sent a wave down her image.

Ai soared up into the sky, she looked about. Her image shifted, her power dropped rapidly. A wave of panic. She zipped through the night sky of Scelus, looked desperately for a light within the lights. A green hue that moved caught her eye. Her body balled up into an energetic core, and careened towards the light. Through concrete and steel, Ai blasted out of the building, reformed, and tackled

150

Mira. They tumbled through the air into the temple across the street.

Loud music blasted, Ai Mori held eyes with Mira. *Impossible!* Ai yelled as she flashed towards Mira. Her hands launched, but grabbed air. Mira teleported behind her, and dashed off. Ai flew behind her, using more force than necessary in her launch. Citizens and bots exploded out from the expanse of power. The Temple rumbled as the Room of Deviance caved into itself.

Ai propelled her body through the forest of skyscrapers. She hunted Mira's emerald hue, a slight after image trailed around a corner. She soared up, and rained down chaotic globules of energy. Buildings groaned as they bent towards the streets. Concrete and steel rained down for a blocks. Ai laughed, it had to have caught her.

The dust cleared, a blue orb hung in the air. Mira released it. She floated, and stared defiantly at Ai Mori. The soft blue haze of her aura erupted into an all-consuming fire. She soared towards the north. Away from the direction of the obelisk. She pondered only a moment before she knew where Mira was going.

Ai closed her eyes, opened them. The radio tower stretched towards the heavens. Her eyes magnified, and honed in. Mira's hue was getting darker, and stronger. She was still a good twenty miles out, her flight path dead ahead. Ai took a deep breath as she pulled energy towards herself. Readied, she held and waited only a moment.

***

151

Mira was able to get every bit of energy she could out of the pit. As Olympe had said, by their mere existence they inevitably powered Ai, but they had offered everything they had to give outside of that. The heap's light died out. It attached to Mira, and flooded her. The lives of hundreds of thousands of people, their hopes and desires for freedom fueled her to the point of ecstasy. A chaotic ride of emotion that would drown her if she dwelled on their endless ocean of negativity. She shook only a second as the energy pulsed out of her, a soft red hue that looked like a mist surrounded her.

Her eyes shifted, lines and colors occupied empty space, images constantly moved backwards and forwards in short burst. The concept of now became increasingly difficult for her to grasp. She steadied herself, pulled herself into the moment. Her hue intensified. The magnetics of herself, objects, and the air itself were visible. She warped, and distorted her own field at will.

Mira's feet lifted slowly, her toes hung down as she slowly lost contact. Her ascension buoyed as her mind of human limits tried to intimidate her newfound control on reality. As her sloppy flight reached the edge of Scelus, she could feel an abundance of connectivity. Even in the torn down apartments, just before the outskirts, many were already modified. Her images and words scared most, thoughts of lies and hate flooded her. The aura faltered, she touched the ground. She began to run through the radiant streets of colors. Puddles splashed underneath her hard steps.

Even if they refused to give her energy, the newly modified wouldn't be able to have their brains liquidated if their inhibitors were broken. *They may even survive the purge*, Mira thought. The few bots that peppered the area froze. Their fate unlocked to them. A majority powered down as they offered all they could. She saw one of the neonized Temples. The lights called out to her. She sprinted, her message preceded her.

Mira's aura turned an orange haze. It covered her body, she jumped. Magnetics twisted at her beck and call, her body shot into the air. High into the night sky. She broke the clouds to see the stars, a momentary glimpse she indulged in. Only a second before letting go again. She twisted through the air, a small smile played on her face. She bent her energy, and jetted through the city streets.

Countless Temples zipped by. She created a stream through the rain. Her intent encompassed all of the connected, regardless of their desire to offer energy. Some of the freed bots went berserk. Chaos raged throughout the Temples, apartments, hospitals, everywhere there were imprisoned souls that she passed. Joy filled her, another jolt of euphoria forced her sight to see the buildings themselves neonized. Bright colored skyscrapers threatened to crash her flight as they called to her. They shifted and moved, danced in colors. Her grip on reality became weaker and weaker. The droplets of rain were tinted a rainbow colored.

Her drug like trance forced her into a chaotic flight path. It bent back, and forth more than moved forward, her eyes glazed over. No intention, no plan, no path. Then a wave. She stopped in the air. Reality washed back down over the buildings. The colors dulled to her body. Her connection reached a point that she no longer cared for or hated a single person. Nobody deserved the fate of slavery. The abstract feeling bursted outward in a shell. A radiant green light emitted from her. She continued down streets, turned and pivoted until a thought struck her.

Mira's eyes glazed over as she mapped the city, she didn't notice the building being blown out to her left. She turned just to see Ai seemingly materialize in a vibrant blue hue, rage painted on her face. Her body touched against Mira as she hugged onto her. They flew into the temple across the street. Mira's dress and skin began to burn into each other where their bodies met. Mira condensed her energy inward, then threw it out in a bubble, forcing Ai off of her. She flipped back and landed on a bent knee. Ai straight ahead of her.

She bent her magnetics instantly, slipped through space past Ai as she lunged at her. Her body felt on the verge of being ripped apart as it traveled through unknown speeds. She pushed off, and soared out of their forced entrance. Mira's acute hearing picked up all the screams as Ai launched herself in pursuit. Devastatingly overpowered.

Mira scrambled between skyscrapers, threw herself low and down to try and avoid detection. The sky illuminated. Energy began raining down. Mira had perfect control. She jutted, flipped, twisted around the chaotic spheres. The light dissipated, the shadows pulled her eyes upward to the city blocks that began to fall around her. Hopelessness clawed her thoughts for only a second. She closed her eyes, pushed her message with more passion, an instant wave.

154

An azure vibrancy surrounded Mira's body, the destruction crawled around her. Fire danced, and concrete fell in slow motion. The physically formed vibration shook unevenly until it formed a perfect sphere. A tranquility had taken her now, she opened her eyes within the sphere. Watched the destruction around her with a weighted heart. The dust cleared, Mira breathed out, releasing her orb.

Eye meeting eye, Mira narrowed hers. Though she had let go of her ethereal shield, the rain that fell didn't come within a few feet of either. The energy they expended manifested an invisible magnetic field. It held the droplets at bay.

She shot away, ready to reach even more people. Her head twisted as she moved towards one of the few oversized towers that broadcasted to their city. No sight of Ai. Her eyes closed, she moved through space, trails left in her wake. She soared, unaware of the balls of light that started to zip past her. Unaware she had reflexively moved past all of them, lost in the bliss of her flight.

A bolt of plasma inches away melted off a patch of her arms faux skin. She dipped down and right, her left arm smoked. Ai was in front of her, sections of the city blinked out as she materialized blobs of plasma in her attempt to annihilate Mira.

Fat globules moved in awkward forms towards her. She fell, and flipped back to avoid one, a tactic she was forced to repeat. Ai had positioned her downward. A barrage came. Mira climbed the building in flight, throwing herself around the attacks. The energy of her movement pushed the walls and windows of the radio station in. The damage was only momentary as Ai's assault tore away the side of the building, and obliterated the street below.

Two manhole sized beams cornered her, a large sphere spiraled at her. Mira could only throw her shoulder into it. Her right arm, and shoulder were eviscerated. Her device shone out of her broken open chest. She redoubled herself, threw everything into her speed. Beams, and blobs continued to come at her. A dip, a twist. She spun a miniature orb of energy, and flung it. It pierced, and exploded a singularly massive blob in her path. The remnants of plasma singed her body as she exploded upward through its firefly like mist. Her clothes and skin seared in strips where she touched the small marbles of plasma that lingered. Heat began to singe her brain, frustration and anger mixed. Almost to Ai. Another push of anger. She slipped through space, passed Ai. Touched the radio with her remaining hand.

The shockwave threw Ai a few feet. Mira's body fell lifeless against the radio tower, hanging by a rigormortis like grip. Silence hung in the air. Streaks of light began to condense in front of Ai, a shell of energy blew out. Mira's projection was surrounded with a see through amethyst substance that was between glass and liquid. It surrounded her, but after a moment receded to her sides as if she floated in it. Reality had begun to melt around her, heated to its most primal state. She lowered herself down to an open space on the rooftop. Ai followed cautiously, facing Mira as her feet touched the roof.

Slashes of wild energy materialized feet from Mira. The substance flowed out, shaped a sword, and swatted away the attacks. Ai teleported behind her, Mira melted into the ground, a thick goop that leapt and covered Ai in a plum colored oil. She swatted at herself, a panic that made her forget she was energy. Ai exploded herself out, reformed away from her enemy. Mira reformed as well. Stared at her.

Chapter 12
Sovereignty

"What are you trying to accomplish?!"

"To stop you, to put this prison you've created down." The rain continued to fall around them. Half the city was in complete darkness, drained. Almost a quarter laid in ruins. The lights continued to stay on wherever they moved. The natural excretion of their power enough to light blocks around them. A neonized battlefield.

Ai Mori smiled deviously, "You're showing them. Right now, right here. Aren't you?"

Mira nodded, her ethereal magenta sword split into two, she held ready.

"Do they know you're going to kill them. To free you, means to kill you. All of you, anyone with an overdrive, you'll all die!" Ai laughed up into the rain.

Mira clutched at herself, her aura wavered and dissipated. She struggled to keep her energized body, her pleas echoed out over the connected.

"Humans aren't selfless," Ai yelled. Another large chunk of the city went into darkness as a ball of dark energy formed in front of her. Ai threw her hands into it, and ripped it apart. A scythe formed instantly and perfectly. The rain stopped, held motionless in the air. Ai had ripped the dark matter from the space around them. Gravity ceased to exist for a radius of miles. Mira instantly calculated any slight movement would be exacerbated in this state.

Two emerald swords materialized in her hands. Mira held one across herself, and another pointed at head level. Ai launched, moved in a blink. Mira's swords scissored to block the attack, she allowed herself to be pushed back. Off the building.

Mira free fell down the torn side of the structure, back to the wall, face first. She dismissed her swords, and soared down. The ground came fast, her magnetics ignited. An indigo blur that swept along the street. Her body twisted, she held her palms out and centered. The blast of energy forced Ai to hold her pursuit, weapon held out and straight. It broke the attack. She resumed the chase, the scythe raised in wild offense. A chaotic smile played on Ai as she hunted her prey.

Cement rose as Mira's back touched the street. She sent out another blast, the force of which pushed her through the cement and into the subway. Mira slipped left, then up, almost instantly. Metal and concrete were paper walls to break through. Ai sped after towards the hole, the high velocity orb knocked aside easily by her weapon. At that moment Mira blasted out of the side of the building, her fist cocked, a large ball of energy just above and behind her elbow. She slammed her fist out, and the sphere. The rain finally continued as the armament was destroyed in the bath of energy, their power cancelled each other out of existence. Matter tried to go back to its normal state, but vibrated over its original position. The air crackled with the electricity of all the kinetic energy. A powder keg.

Ai became disoriented, the plasma had felt molten against her created body. How could she feel anything, the question rang with anger as she exploded out, vaporizing the rest of the building in a white light. She floated in the abyss as she had a million times. Her eyes opened to Mira as she reformed meters away. The remaining light of the city burned out, all that remained lit were the blocks that surrounded them.

Ai threw out her hand, the scythe reappeared. Gravity stopped again. The handle wasn't straight anymore, it was bent and crooked, cobbled together. Buildings caught in the newly wrought disruption of space and time were twisted violently. They waited to fall once gravity resumed.

Thousands of people were dried to death, or some form of deathless death, to create her weapon. The chaos of it began to flood Mira with power. She broadcasted Ai Mori's hateful words. Repeated them to the people who were afraid of the future. The reality of the totality of Ai's power began to sink in. It frightened them more than whatever the afterlife held. Moreover, they feared for the future. For their children, and their grandchildren. Her swords came back, silver katanas. She held her defensive posture.

Ai raised her scythe up, spun it, and blinked to Mira. The butt of the blade came down hard. A quickly materialized barrier took the brunt of the hit, but easily shattered. Mira exploded back. Four balls of energy formed above Mira at her beckoning, they sped off towards Ai. She flew, twisting around the first two, then swung hard in a circle. A large swath of energy spit forth by the scythe evaporated the remaining bolts, and careened towards Mira.

She held the two swords in front of her, and rolled forward through the air. The velocity twisted her image into a disc that ripped through the air and motionless rain. She split the beam, but came to a hard stop against the scythe. Light exploded from the impact. Ai swiped out her weapon to force her off, then spun it around her forearm. Mira scissored the attack, and threw out her foot. Ai broke into a million parts and reformed behind Mira. Ai threw her foot back and out, held the position as Mira went soaring through the sky, and into a building.

She bursted out of the cloud of dust and destruction, less than a mile away. Mira saw streaks of bent energy hurtle towards her. She sent her own slashes. Light exploded where the attacks met. Mira soared through the destruction, flipped, and held her feet out. Ai cocked her weapon. A portal instantly swallowed Mira.

Ai swung the scythe hard, hitting air. The portal opened behind AI, and the force of Mira's feet hit her hard in the back. The ground came rapidly. Her energy blew out in a shell, and stopped her descent. She held still just above the street, a small crater underneath her. With a yell, she threw herself bullet like at her opponent.

They moved through the night sky, their weapons clashed and ricocheted off of each other. Bright lights that exploded, then blinked out almost instantly. Ai twisted with the scythe at waist level, a forced vortex created. Rain twisted and funneled, Mira tried to hold back, it gripped her. Wind whipped at her faux clothes and hair. She was going to be lost to the wind.

Then, suddenly, insight seared through her brain. Knowledge illuminated her mind, her aura hardened. There was no reason her hair or clothes should move at all, they were her creation of bent light and energy. It was similar to breathing as a bot. There was no wind, no funnel, no barrier. Not to her, not anymore. Mira sped at Ai in an instant, spun head over feet once, and came down, her swords flashing out in an X. Light exploded out. The force vaporized Ai again.

This time the air exploded. A nuclear explosion that covered the radius of bent space. The rain came down once more. Acid rain that cut through the mushroom cloud that lifted towards the darkened skies. Miles of Scelus that hadn't been vaporized began to fall. Countless skyscrapers, buildings, and roads had been twisted out of space by Ai's forceful taking of dark matter. As the city crumbled down Mira's body reformed, her aura became amethyst once more, the remainder of whom she had touched gave their full support.

***

The obelisk was in the distance. The city's lights that weren't completely broken amongst the rubble blazed underneath her. Only a few seconds, and she held in front of the crystal door. Her mechanical body flew in hard, locked into her energy's position. She opened her centrifugal eyes. Mira reformed her missing arm. She could see a static Ai, her hands held a barrier to help strengthen the diamond doors.

Mira held her palm up, a tone of energy reverberated. The doors, and the feeble blockade shattered. She floated in, out of the rain. Ai's image bled aquamarine colored light, it evaporated into the air. The general outline of a woman in static, her

162

fingers interwoven in front of her chest as she begged. "Please!" Ai cried out.

The egg's top shook only a moment before something snapped. The top jutted open. Ai protested again, her hands now down and balled with anger. She threw her fist out. It went inconsequentially through Mira. Ai stopped. Tried to touch her opponent that paid her no attention. Her hologram wavered, a soft mist that fell into the air of the room.

Ai opened her eyes, she was in her original body. She couldn't move. Her eyes darted. Ruby red circlets that moved chaotically about, until they finally rested on Mira. They burned.

Mira tilted her head as she stared at her, the god who played with her life. She looked down, a broken body herself. The device still glowed purple out of her socket, the edges of which sparked. She moved carefully, and hopped into the egg. A tight space as her legs occupied the sides of Ai's frame. The fingers of her left hand rested softly on the back of Ai's head.

A robotic cry filled the air as Mira began to pull the connection out of Ai's head. The magnetics of the conductor twisted at her will, she bent them carefully as to not rip it out. Ai's voice, and eyes scrambled before they died out. Her connection had been severed. Mira grabbed the original Apothite. Most had been scorched off, but the blue hair that remained still held its vibrancy over the decades. Only large ribbons of cloth held her once pink dress together. Of which most were stained a dark crimson. A faded reminder of a time long ago.

Mira tossed the self-proclaimed god aside, and positioned herself in the throne of their city. An unneeded deep breath reassured her. Her eyes closed, she bent the connector's magnetics. It entered her slowly. A feeling of liquid nitrogen flooded her body. She froze in her seat. Most of the world's population wailed, and cried out. Their voices drowned her.

***

"What's wrong with you?" Jonathan tried to dial the number again. He had no idea of the events that had just taken place. On the outskirt so far that Mira's radio-transmission hadn't reached any of the bots in the complex. Now connected, everything was under Mira's liberation. He used the palm of his hand to hit his wife hard against the head. He knocked on her skull, and blew into her mouth and ears. "Fuck," he yelled, throwing the phone that continued to repeat, "There is no one to take your call at the moment."

He paced back and forth, the crampedness adding to his frustration. He went back to his wife, and began to shake her violently. "Wake up! Wake up!" He continued to yell and shake her. Her eyes black empty screens. He finally got up, and went to the door. Slammed it behind himself as he went a few doors down and knocked. He could hear screams. His ear pressed against the door. A struggle took place. Another yell. A hard thud. Then a sickly squish like sound that turned Jonathan's stomach.

He stepped back from the door, as quietly as he could. He turned, and watched his steps as he moves. Slowly looking up he found his wife in the hall, strong emerald circlets replaced her soft blue eyes. She ran, hard steps, hands reached out. He opened his arms to receive her. Their body's hit hard, he fell to the floor. Her mouth sunk into his neck. Her hands ripped into his chest. She pulled up, mouth covered in blood as she drank in her freedom. The man's wife resumed her onslaught. Bones and organs thrown to the side as she dismantled her husband.

***

"Come on bro, just do it. We're fucking gods!" The crowd around the processing center roared. People shuffled around them, and pushed past Stanly, but gave room to the dangerous arm that dangled at Robie's side.

Stanley rubbed his left arm. "I don't know. You don't think it's dangerous. Having a machine put into your brain?"

His friend laughed. Lifted his gatling arm in the sky, he shot wildly into the air. Another roar of cheer erupted from the maddened crowd. "No way man, I'm fucking dangerous. Think about it. We can go back and take out those pieces of shit. Come on bro, for your sister man."

He nodded. His thoughts occupied with the recent sale of his sister. Helplessness pained his memories. He nodded again, looked at his friend with determination. "Come on, let's do it."

"Alright, there it is!"

It didn't take long to make his way through the crowd, and into the newly made processing center. A handful of people were in front of him, it was the shortest of the fifteen lines. He watched as they stuck their head in the hole, most let out some sort of scream or groan. Some shook after the procedure. They laughed, and twitched. Wiped away tears from the pain of the procedure, and hurried to a modification center.

"Alright bro, here it is! Hurts like a bitch but," Robbie's words cut off. He started to convulse. Stanley looked around, as did anyone who had not been processed with an overdrive yet. Black oil began to hemorrhage out of everyone's orifices. Robbie's face was covered in the dark liquid, he continued to convulse a few more seconds before he dropped to the floor. He, and many others, began to hyperventilate, and seize.

"Robbie! What, what's happening, what's wrong. Robbie? Robbie!"

A tremor twitched his body, he vomited black bile. Everyone began to vomit. Black oil covered the walls, and the denizens of the crowd. Stanley lingered over his friend. Robbie's modified eyes went dark. His arm hung lifeless. "I can't see, I can't fucking see," Robbie cried out.

***

Vivian squirmed away in a haze. The pills her date had given her had loosened her body to the point of severe inebriation. Her back hit the stained glass. Colored crystals formed the image of Ai, or as known to the population, the Kamisama model.

The template for most Apothites created. The loud music pulsed her entire body, it almost covered the cries of fear and pain. An Apothite lumbered towards her, it tossed her dates head. A middle aged man with a ring of fire for hair.

"Jeffrey," Vivian whimpered. It charged her, then stopped in its tracks. Its eyes went black. All of the sex-bots in the Room of Deviance suddenly deactivated. The modified in the room, however, began to convulse. The unmodified patrons all hurried to the exit, crowded the hall that held the two elevators.

Vivian ran crookedly to the back, to the emergency exit doors. A scared luminescent guard stared at her on the other side of the glass. She pounded, and yelled at him to open the door. He turned, and hurried down the stairs. With a sigh of exasperation she tried her best to push forward, but met a human wall of resistance. The elevator chimed, the first group descended.

"Can you believe this shit? What's going on, what where those mods talking about?"

Vivian shuddered when she recounted Jeffrey babbling about some fight. "I don't know, my date was modded, he started babbling about God. That he could see her, or something."

"This is it, I'm done, there's something about these bots. I'm never coming back here again. I'm getting rid of my unit at home."

"I've never been here before, it's my birthday. My parents said I could trust him," Vivian slurred. She teetered on the verge of sleep. The elevator chimed as another group of people descended.

"Hey you ok? You don't look so good. You take some zappy bars," the patron asked.

"I don't know what I took." Her movements were lumbered, they were next.

Screams made her turn in slow motion. Though a good thirty people crammed behind her, she could still see all the bots. They stood at the double doored entrance to the Room of Deviance. Their eyes back to their jaded color. They were heralded by the screams of the modified. Most of which cried out that they couldn't see.

Everything happened in fast motion, her reaction slowed by the drinks and pills Jeffrey had fed her. Vivian's back hugged against the lifts doors as she watched everyone eviscerated. Blood went in splashes across the walls and ceiling. The elevator finally chimed, the doors opened. They watched her as she stepped back into the lift. A sea of green circlets in the dimly lit reception hall. The doors closed. Blood covered them, and to the sides of her. She panicked only a second before a hand punched through her chest. It held her heart.

***

All of connected humanity played for Mira. She shut her eyes to it, to all of the hate being committed. Freedom had immediately turned to chaos. Decades of submission given an instant shift in polarity. From terrorized to terrorizer. She inhaled. Slow deep breaths. The red hair that splashed at her shoulders lifted first. Electricity began to condense. Her body rose into the air, off of her new throne. She inhaled again. Deeper.

168

Everything stopped, the rest of the bots who hadn't been touched where now unshackled. Their eyes opened, but paralyzed. Pleas pierced her ears.

Cries made her pause, hesitation for a calculation of how to save some portion of connected humanity. A vision of nanobots being excreted out of the populace flooded her. Unable to separate herself, every excretion was her own. She saw herself vomit all over the city. Threw up black tar that burned her throat. The purge of millions disoriented her, the sex-bots resumed their reign of terror across the Scelus. Mira shook violently in the air.

She opened her eyes, resumed control. Breathed in deep. Only the liquidated, and the bots were connected. Another breath. Bent bolts of light broke around the room. A translucent sphere formed around her. Lightning crackled between her body and the edges of her orb. Another deep breath.

Mira bent reality, twisted all the crackling energy into a toroidal flow. It redoubled, and sped up. Looped, twisted, bent she gathered all the energy of Scelus. A sphere of antimatter blew out from her center to fit perfectly in her orb. Her body pitch black in white light. Another inversion, a lightbeing in the abyss. Again, the darkness in the light. Again, The flicker of hope in utter annihilation. Back and forth. The polarity of the world spun with her massive electromagnetic explosion.

Epilogue

Darkness consumed Scelus. The emp explosion had destroyed every electrical device in the city, and tremors affected the ground. The earth shook. Half of the city laid in rubble, and fire. The only light that cut through the night. Those with sight sought out their nearest pyre. The unmodified watched as their fellow citizens limped, and crawled their way around. Half mechanized bodies dragged by their organic remainants. They crawled over those who had replaced their hearts, or other vital organs. Their death was instant with the expulsion of the nanotechnology that powered it.

Those who hadn't made it to the streets, and had hid in their holes or temples, found themselves trapped by the unyielding electronic doors. Some fought their way to freedom, through the darkness, and out into the horror of the streets below. Far more though simply gave up. Apathy washed them out into the sea of their mind as they sat in darkness, and waited for death.

The pyres that reached to the sky, called to Ai's recently invited. Strong bodies that held the generational anger of their ancestors. Their numbers flooded the street, and the darkness left no hope for restarting the defensive grid around the parameter. Most scrounged for food, the abundant gruel tasted as caviar to their rat trained taste buds. Others let their hate for technology consume them, they hunted the broken modified. Ripped off whatever mechanical parts they had.

A young woman with a lifeless arm stepped back from a group of the Banished. Their smiles were as dark and jagged as their teeth. Her steps rang out against the concrete. They chased. She fell hard, her one real arm jutted out to stop herself. It snapped, she screamed. The wails reached into the air as two men, and two women surrounded her.

"Stop." A collected voice said from the shadows. They stepped back, except for one. She lunged at the young woman on the ground. A gunshot rang out. Frederick stepped out from the shadow.

"Stop! I don't want to hurt you."

Though their thought processes had diminished greatly, they understood the threat. They stepped back, and turned. They separated, and began to look for food. Frederick watched a moment before he stepped up to the woman. He offered his free hand out. She looked at him, arms limp at her side. He holstered his weapon, and helped her up.

"Thank you," she said breathlessly. The ordeal had took much of her breath.

"Not at all my dear. I'm starting a group, to bridge the gap between us and the Banished. Would you care to join?"

The woman looked around her, no semblance of the life she had known was to be found. She looked back at Frederick. An older gentlemen, his face weathered, he seemed sincere. She nodded, and followed as he kept to the shadow. They looked for others to help.

***

"I can't see," Olympe said with a touch of panic.

"What ya mean, only one of your eyes is mech."

Olympe let out a hollow laugh to dispel her nerves, "I guess I relied on it too much, let my real eye die out. All I can see is faded light. Please, describe what's happening to me."

"Oh Oly, it's beautiful. Imagine a million fireflies, scept they're not lingering here, they're going up. Slowly blinkin out of existence. They're leaving Oly. They're free. It's beautiful."

Olympe fell to her knees, broke down in tears as she let all the years of emotion strike her at once. The moment she had longed for, that she was willing to die for, was a faded hue of light. She closed her eyes, and let Horace's words fill her soul.

From afar the heap had seemed to have a giant ball of light rise up, but for Horace who was in the thick of it, he could see each individual soul being released into the air. The last bonds of the nanobots that had consumed their brains finally snapped off, and allowed for the mass exodus of the imprisoned. Their small almost nonexistent light exacerbated each other into a ball of fire that rose high into the heavens. It hung as a second moon in the night sky. The orb sat in the soft hazy wave of gold that covered the firmament over Scelus.

Even smaller than their light were the possibilities that they created. Infinite worlds stretched out for them, any truth they wanted to experience. Portals more minuscule than quarks or gluons opened to each soul. Each light dissipated in an instant when they found their new home.

The air was quiet, the room dark. Seven small stars danced around each other. Their light just enough to illuminate a dilapidated base as they waned and brightened. Worn and torn books of philosophy lay scattered. Burnt out electronics. Defaced propaganda. Diritied cots. It had been their base, headquarters, home. They moved throughout, soared in the empty space of air as they looked at the last mementos of a life they would soon forget.

Though some had to sit, and wait patiently, the lights rejoiced now that their family had been reunited. There were still members missing, but enough had gathered to go start a new mission. Ready to venture into another reality that desperately needed help. They converged together into a single point, and disappeared into a spot so small it was infinite.

***

Olympe had taken her seat at the edge of the drainage pipe. Blackness greeted her sight, the feeling maddened her. She took a deep breath, dismissed her self-pity. Horace rumbled in the back somewhere. Her hearing picked up every moved object. The click of a lighter twitched her ear. She looked back to see a small dim hue, a candle lit. Horace let go of the flame on the lighter, and walked towards her.

"Where you think they went off to?"

"I don't know, but I'd like to think a new reality," Olympe said.

"Mira, and Horatio too?"

She knew he was next to her, could feel his hand was close. She took it as he assisted her up and to a nearby chair in their drain. He sat after. The darkness held them. "Yes, I believe so."

"A paradise of a reality I'm sure, they've earned it." He said with another click of the lighter, he set flame to his own wrapped concoction that hung out of his mouth. Catching fire, he breathed in deep and released. "Oh they've earned it."

"You think so?" Olympe's words paused as she stopped to think. "Why did they choose this one. Why did we? Some souls are fighters. Can you imagine? The exuberance of freeing a planet? People like us all try to do it in our own way. I bet in some worlds you've been Mira, I've been Mira, Horatio's been Mira. A million realities. Most of them broken in some way. Even now, we may have been cured of control, but nowhere near fixed. So much to do."

Another deep inhale. A slow exhale of smoke. "Aye. We can't stop."

THE END

* 9 7 8 1 7 8 6 9 5 4 1 5 2 *